One Strange Summer

I hope your summer isn't as STRANGE as Maybeline's! But I do hope you enjoy this book! Happy Reading!

—Jewell ♡

Copyright © 2021 Jewell Anne Sandy

All rights reserved.

ISBN: 9798593200723

The first person who comes to mind when I think of this book is my dear Uncle Kaine. I remember my last conversation with you, I was telling you about my notebook full of stories and you said you would love to read it. That phone conversation ended with Mudr holding the phone to my mouth like a microphone while I played your favorite Phoebe Buffay song on my ukulele—the one about building a snowman then finding her mom dead in the kitchen. I was writing the thirty-third chapter of this very book in my notebook on my bed while my mother made taco soup in the kitchen when we found out what had happened. I hope that you are happy in your afterlife.

Pippi loves you forever.

Table of Contents

Chapter 1 — 1
Chapter 2 — 5
Chapter 3 — 9
Chapter 4 — 13
Chapter 5 — 16
Chapter 6 — 20
Chapter 7 — 24
Chapter 8 — 28
Chapter 9 — 33
Chapter 10 — 37
Chapter 11 — 40
Chapter 12 — 44
Chapter 13 — 48
Chapter 14 — 52
Chapter 15 — 57
Chapter 16 — 61
Chapter 17 — 64
Chapter 18 — 68
Chapter 19 — 71
Chapter 20 — 74
Chapter 21 — 78
Chapter 22 — 82

Chapter 23	85
Chapter 24	90
Chapter 25	94
Chapter 26	97
Chapter 27	102
Chapter 28	105
Chapter 29	109
Chapter 30	112
Chapter 31	116
Chapter 32	122
Chapter 33	128
Chapter 34	134
Chapter 35	141
Chapter 36	146
Chapter 37	152
Chapter 38	158
Chapter 39	164
Chapter 40	169
Chapter 41	174
Chapter 42	181
Chapter 43	185
Chapter 44	190
Chapter 45	197
Chapter 46	200

Chapter 47	206
Chapter 48	212
Chapter 49	218
Chapter 50	223
Chapter 51	228
Chapter 52	233
Chapter 53	237
Chapter 54	242

<u>Chapter 1</u>

Beep, beep, beep, beep....

I pulled my pillow up over my ears, trying to block out the sound of my annoying alarm clock, and at the same time praying it would just turn off on its own.

I groaned and rolled onto my stomach. The clock kept beeping.

Suddenly, the room was flooded with light. "Wake up, sleepyhead," a voice said. "You're going to be late for work."

I rolled over and set the pillow down. "Can't they find someone else to work the coffee machine?"

"With your boss?" Marcie smiled at me. "You're lucky you were able to take just a week off. Come on. You need to get up or we're both going to be late." She left my room. I slumped back down on my bed.

I'm not a morning person. I hate getting up in the morning. Once I get going, I'm fine, but it's the process of getting there that I don't like.

Marcie on the other hand is always one step ahead of the game. She picks out her clothes the night before, she schedules out her whole day on her phone, why, she even preps her breakfast as a precaution with her obsession with not being late for anything (as if she'd need it)!

"If you're not out here by the time I'm out the door...." I could hear Marcie grabbing her keys from the kitchen.

I rolled my head around and looked at the clock. "It's seven eleven!" I yelled to her.

"You can never be too early," she said. "Now come on! I'm leaving...."

I sighed and twisted my body so that my feet fell on the floor. "Hang on," I said groggily and staggered into the kitchen.

"Now, can I count on you to get to work on time?" she said, standing with her hand ready on the doorknob.

"Yes, Marcie," I said, sitting down at the counter. I picked up my phone. She reached over and took it out of my hand.

"Actually get around," she said to me.

I rolled my eyes and stood up. I walked around the island to her and held out my hand. She held my phone away from me. "You can have this back when you're done getting around."

"So what? You're going to stay here until I'm all

ready for work?"

"No, I'm not going to be late for class." She scanned me with her piercing green eyes as if I should have known that. I probably should have. "I'm going to set it here"—she set it on the counter on the other side of the refrigerator—"and you aren't going to touch it until you're completely, completely, completely ready to walk out the door." Did she really have that much faith I'd be obedient?

"I'll see you later, Maybeline," she said. She opened the door to our apartment and left for her class.

I immediately retrieved my phone from the counter and leaned against the island.

It wasn't until sometime after scrolling through a million Instagram posts that I looked up at the clock in the corner of my phone screen and saw it was 7:43. Holy guacamole! I quickly set my phone down and hurried to get ready for work.

I hastily poured orange juice into a glass and was about to pour cereal in a bowl when I realized that would take too long to eat. I took my orange juice with me into my room and drank it while I got dressed. Then I hurried into the bathroom to brush my teeth. I looked at the clock. 7:49. I quickly combed through my tangled brown hair—so fast that it hurt. I knew I didn't have time to do full make-up, so I just put on a layer of eyeliner and called it good. 7:54. Would I really make it on time?

I grabbed my purse and a bagel from the fridge and hurried out the door. I went downstairs and got to my car. I couldn't find the keys! I'd practically dumped all the contents out of my purse onto the passenger seat before I found them. I quickly started the car. The clock on the dash read 7:57. There's no way I'd make it now. I pulled out of the parking lot and tried to get there as fast as I could without getting pulled over for speeding.

Chapter 2

"Sorry I'm late," I said breathlessly as I hurried into the coffee shop.

"Chevy, there you are," my boss, Mr. Saperstien, said. "Come on, we've got customers waiting." He went into the back room. I was surprised he hadn't reprimanded me right then, but I figured he just wanted me to get to work as soon as possible and that I would get it later.

I went back and set my purse down and retrieved my apron and name tag. I walked back out of the back room and stood behind the cash register to take orders. Mr. Saperstien was right; we had a lot of customers that morning! Either that, or they'd just piled up over time because there was no one on duty to take their orders.

I think I'd filled at least a quadrillion orders before I finally had a break in the coffee traffic. It was already 9:12. What a morning this has been already!

I was brushing my hands off on my apron when I heard someone clear his throat.

"Can I have a large espresso, no caffeine?" his gruff voice demanded.

"Oh, yeah, sure, just a minute," I said, and went back to the coffee machine and filled a cup for him. "That'll be three twenty-nine," I said as I handed it to him. He gave me four dollars. When I finished counting out change I said, "Have a good day," but he just ignored me and left. Oh well. As long as the customer's happy, they say.

"Maybeline, there you are!" A frantic young woman came into the shop. "I've been trying to get a hold of you all morning!" She sat at the counter in front of me.

"Sorry, Maria," I said. Maria's my older sister of three years. We look almost exactly alike, except for her dark hair is short and permed while mine is long and straight. Another difference between us is Maria's eyes are the color of sweet creamy chocolate, while mine are the color of sparkling blue waterfalls.

"Seriously," she continued, "I've called your phone a dozen times today. Why won't you pick up?"

Oh, right. My phone. I remembered I'd left it on the kitchen counter. "Sorry, I must have forgotten it at home," I said.

"Rough first day back to work, huh?" Her lips finally curved up in a smile.

"Yeah," I sighed.

"Well, I'll forgive you…," Maria said with a twinkle in her eye, "…if you'll serve me a nice iced coffee."

"All right." I returned her smile. I continued to talk to her as I made her order. "What was it you were trying to call me about?"

"Oh yeah," she said. "Mom wants to know if you've got anyone to go with to the community dance in July."

"Why didn't she just ask me instead of sending you to?"

"'Cause," she said, "you never talk to Mom about boys—"

"Yeah, well, moms shouldn't get involved in their daughters' love lives!" I said. Maria smirked at me. "Oh, I see now," I said. I handed her her coffee.

"Thanks," she said. "So, do you?"

"I don't know!" I said. "I'm not a boy-magnet like you are! Who knows if I'll have a boyfriend by then?" It was true. With Maria's excellent fashion sense and perfectly tanned long legs, she could be on the cover of *Victoria's Secret,* easy.

"I am not a boy-magnet," she said.

"You are too!" I said.

"I'm just as much a boy-magnet as you, Maybeline," she replied.

"Oh come on. You've had, what, *six* boyfriends now?"

"Yeah, and you've had, uh…."

"Two," I finished for her. "Brady and Rick. And those weren't even serious. I'm talking about serious!"

"What about Bruce Combs? You were *totally* serious about him."

"Bruce Combs was just all a big mistake!" I can't believe she'd brought *him* up.

"Still, you were serious about him…."

Chapter 3

After we'd finally finished arguing—well, I can't really say my sister and I ever finish an argument; we just yell at each other until our fight energy burns out and we just disagree in silence—Maria left because she had a class at her university at 11:30—I felt like I was the only one who didn't go to a college, but I wasn't sure what I wanted to go into yet so I didn't really have any reason to attend anyway. The coffee shop wasn't very busy at this hour, so I only had a few orders to fill.

When 12:00 came around, the place got busier as everyone was on lunch break. Because of this, mine actually wasn't until 1:00.

I stumbled some through the lunch crowd but I survived. Now came 1:00, our least busy hour, so I could hang up my apron for a short while and rest.

I looked around the empty little store and sighed in pleasure. I looked down at my waist and untied my apron.

I guess while I was preoccupied with my apron, another customer had entered the place and had been lost in my oblivion. I looked up and gasped, and I guess I must have jumped a little too because I knocked a stack of pastries over on the counter. And while I was reaching to pick those up, I knocked over the muffin stand too, and in a frantic reflex managed to spill bags of coffee beans on the floor behind the counter.

"Oh no no no no," I said, looking at the mess at my feet. I would have to get a broom to sweep it up. I looked back up. Oh no, and there was a customer too! That's right; that's what had startled me and caused me to knock the stuff over in the first place. He looked back at me with shock on his face. He probably thought I was a bit of a psycho.

"Here, let me help you with that," he said, picking up some of the little muffins and setting them upright on their stand, which he'd righted as well.

"Thanks," I said, picking up the pastries. I turned down to the mess at my feet.

"Here." He walked around the counter and grabbed a broom that was leaning against a wall and came over to help me.

"Actually, I'm not sure you're supposed to be back here…," I said.

"Nonsense. I'll be back where I'm supposed to be

by the time you finish making me a cappuccino," he said, gathering the dark dusty mess together.

"All right," I said uncertainly. And he was right. While I had my back to him, he'd finished cleaning up my mess and set the broom back in its original spot before returning to his place on the customers' side of the counter.

"Here you go," I said, handing him his coffee. "Sorry about the delay and everything."

"It's all right. I'm in no hurry," he said. "Besides, everyone has an off-day, right?"

I liked this boy. Couldn't he be my boss instead of Mr. Saperstien?

"Yeah, I guess," I said aloud. "You still didn't have to clean up my big disaster."

"Don't mention it," he said, handing me the money, change counted exactly. He held up his hand and left. I waved back just before he'd turned around.

Well, that was lucky, I thought. *What are the odds of a customer being that patient with you as you make mistake after mistake, and then actually go out of their way to help you? -1%.*

I was about to go into the back room when I realized I hadn't packed myself a lunch. Maybe I should start listening to Marcie more often. Well, at least when I got back to my apartment I could grab my phone.

I told Mr. Saperstien I was leaving and he said I need to hurry hurry hurry back! I guess *everyone* knew how reckless and forgettable I was.

When I reached my apartment, I made myself a super-fast peanut butter sandwich with raspberry jam smothered in it.

I picked up my phone.

Only seven missed calls. That wasn't a lot for me.

I texted my mom: *I don't know about boys 4 dance* and quickly ate my PB&J. Mr. Saperstien wouldn't have it if I was late *twice* on my day back to work.

Chapter 4

"Hey," Marcie said as she entered the apartment.

"Hi," I said.

"You decided to come home for lunch?" She set her stuff on the table.

"No," I grumbled. "I forgot to pack myself a lunch." I *hated* admitting I was wrong and she was right.

"I told you you should've packed a lunch last night," she said.

"I know," I groaned.

"Maybe you need to start listening to me more," she replied.

I pretended not to care. She was right, though. I really *did* need to listen to her more.

"Did you make it to work on time?"

"Ugh," was my answer. She understood.

"You know, sometimes I worry about you, Maybeline," she said.

"I worry about me too sometimes," I mumbled.

She laughed. "Maybe I need to start taking your phone with me to my classes until you learn to not let it distract you. That was why you were late, wasn't it?"

"Yeah," I said. "But my sister was trying to get ahold

of me all morning and was freaking out, so that won't work."

"You didn't bring your phone with you to work?" She seemed just as shocked as that boy had been when I'd made a move clumsy enough to embarrass the whole town.

"No, I was in such a hurry I'd forgotten it," I said, putting it in my purse at that moment so I wouldn't make that mistake again.

"Really? How *late* were you?"

"Well...," I said. "Around the time I was supposed to be on my third order, I was just leaving the complex...."

"My god, Maybeline," she said. "What were you doing all morning?"

"What do you think?" I said, briefly removing my phone from the bag over my shoulder to show her.

"Oh, Maybeline...," she laughed. "Maybe I need to start texting you at every stoplight as a reminder that there's a real world outside of Instagram."

"Yeah, maybe," I said. I think she might have been kidding a little, but it *would* be a good thing for her to do. "All right, I'm going to go now," I said, heading for the door.

"You're leaving already?" she said. "But it's only one twenty-three."

"I know," I said.

"Finally listening to me, huh?" She smiled.

I made a face and groaned.

She laughed. "It's for your own good, Maybeline."

"I just don't want Mr. Saperstien to fire me for being late again," I said quickly, pretending I wasn't giving in to her actually great advice and life habits, and left. I knew she was feeling pride for finally getting some sense into me...or had she? Who knew?

I think I might have given Mr. Saperstien a bit of a scare with my entrance at 1:31 because the second his eyes found me, his jaw dropped and he almost let go of the cup he was washing.

"Uh, oh, uh, Chevy," he stuttered. "You're back, um, rather early."

I shrugged. "Yeah, I guess I just got finished with lunch a little bit earlier. Is there anything I can help with?"

The only answer I got was some incoherent stuttering, so I just put on my apron and name tag and waited behind the cash register for any afternoon coffee drinkers.

Chapter 5

The second I opened the door, my whole vision was filled with golden fluff as Coffee Woman's Best Friend greeted me.

"Hey, Bud," I said, scratching him behind his ears where he likes it the most. "Have you been a good boy today?" I was on my knees so I was at eye level with him.

Ruff! he barked and licked my face.

I giggled. "You were?" He barked again. "Aw," I said, giving him kisses of my own.

"How was work?" Marcie asked. "The rest of it, I mean."

"Fine," I replied, petting Buddy and standing up. "Mr. Saperstien wouldn't say a word to me," I said, coming all the way inside and closing the front door.

"How come?" she asked.

"I think he was in shock," I replied. "There was a lot of incoherent stuttering and wide-eyed staring."

"'Cause you've never been early before?"

"Yeah, I think that's it," I said. We both laughed.

"One day out of the two years you've worked there, you're early," she said, smiling and pulling a strand of her red hair from her face.

"Yeah." I smiled. I giggled. "Well, partially. I was *really* late this morning."

"Still, it's something to celebrate," she said. She went over to the microwave to cook dinner.

"What, are we going to toast to it?" I said.

"That's a great idea," she said, clicking the buttons for the correct cook time.

"I was kidding," I said.

"Still, I learned during my psychology class that reward encourages behavior. If we toast to this, you'll probably start being early more often!"

"Wait, you take a psychology class?" I said. "I thought you were going into business."

"I am," she said. "But salesmen—or saleswomen— who have an understanding of that kind of stuff are more likely to sell their product because they'll be able to connect with the customer more."

"Right…," I said. I paused. "What were we talking about again?" Marcie paused too. "You know what, it doesn't matter," I said. "Let's eat."

"Mm mm," I said. "Nothing like good old macaroni straight out of the microwave."

Marcie smiled. "You should let your grandma hear you say that," she said.

"What?" I said. "What's wrong with good old macaroni straight out of the microwave?"

"Well, first of all, it's not old," she said, "and second of all, they actually cooked back then, so I don't think your grandmother would consider it good either."

"Yeah, well, I still think it is," I said, clearing my place at the table. "Hey, I don't think I told you," I said. "The most amazing thing happened today."

"Yeah, you were at work ahead of time," Marcie said. "Which, we still need to celebrate," she added.

"No, I'm talking about something else," I said. "You know how I'm such a klutz?"

"Doesn't everyone?"

I made a face at her. *"No.* Well, I mean, I don't know—but that's not the point! The point is I was being a klutz today at work—"

"Was that before or after you jump-scared Saperstien?"

"Before," I said.

"That's good," she said. "That means you had the perfect afternoon at work."

"Oh, yeah, I guess…," I said. "But that's not the

point of my story. You see, there was this customer there…." And then I told her about how I'd screwed up, but he was still patient and in the best of moods.

"Wow," Marcie said, her mouth full of cookie. Marcie likes to snack while she listens to stories. I think it helps her refrain from interrupting the speaker. "And you thought your sister was the boy-magnet."

"Excuse me?" I said.

"Come on," she said, "just some random guy 'isn't in any hurry' in Buffalo on a weekday? *And* he just helped you? Maybeline, he went behind the counter and *swept.* He cleaned up more of your mess than you did." She put another Oreo in her mouth. "All I'm saying is, *I think somebody likes somebody…."*

"Shut up," I said, taking a pillow from the couch and throwing it at her.

And we had a good old pillow fight that night.

Chapter 6

A few days went by.

I hadn't seen the nice boy who'd helped me since he'd waved at me before leaving with his cappuccino that first day back to work. I was a little disappointed but I wasn't going to let it bring me down. In fact, I do believe this has been the best work week in the history of time. Mr. Saperstien had a newfound respect for me, as I'd been having Marcie help me remember everything and I was feeling so motivated that I hadn't been a single minute late all week. Marcie's been teasing me, saying I just don't want to miss that boy if he comes back for more coffee, but I think it's that reward thing in psychology she was telling me about. I'd been so appreciated and praised well at work, I actually kind of wanted to be there (something I never thought I'd say).

"Great work today, Chevy," Mr. Saperstien said to me as I was gathering my stuff to go.

"Thank you," I replied. "See you tomorrow!"

"Tomorrow? Chevy, it's Friday. I'll see you Monday."

"Oh, right," I said. Why did we have to have weekends again?

* * *

"Ugh," I said as I set my purse down.

"Bad day?" Marcie didn't turn away from the TV.

"No," I said. Buddy was looking up at me, his tail swaying wildly. I reached down to pet him. "Marcie, why do we have to have weekends?"

"'Cause it's against the law to not give your employees days off?" For the first time since I'd gotten home, she looked at me, and I could see she was puzzled. "Since when don't you like days off?"

"I don't know," I said. "I'm just really liking work right now."

She didn't say anything. The somebody-likes-somebody joke was getting very old and I think she was beginning to realize.

"What are you watching?" I asked, coming to the living room.

"News," she sighed. "I'm bored. Well, not anymore, since you're here." She smiled at me.

"Aw, I missed you too." I sat down next to her on the couch and hugged her. She hugged me back. And we stayed like that for a moment. I sometimes felt like she was the big sister I'd never had—well, the other one, at least.

"What are we going to do for supper tonight?" I asked her as we came out of our hug. I glanced at the television screen briefly. Something about animal attacks in the country. I don't know. I didn't really care that much so I looked away.

"Already taken care of," she said, smiling.

"Awesome stuffed crust quadruple cheesy delight from McFeels'!" we both exclaimed.

"Did you get the breadsticks too?" I asked.

"Um, *yeah,*" Marcie said. "What's pizza without breadsticks and dipping sauce?"

"You read my mind, sister!" I said. "Hey, should we watch a movie too? You know, like a fun pizza-movie night?"

"See, Maybeline," she answered, "this is why people need days off. So gal pals can have rocking stay-at-home movie nights! And pedicures," she added.

"Definitely pedicures," I agreed.

"Which movie should we watch?" she asked.

"*Rachel and Damien!*" I said without hesitation.

"You just *really* like that one, don't you?" Marcie teased. I'd probably seen it at least a dozen times.

"Who doesn't love a good old love story?" I said.

"All right...," she said, but I could tell she was just as excited as I was.

I waited with the Blu-ray menu up on the TV before the pizza came so that we would enjoy them both at the same time, not a minute without the other. As soon as we'd both sat down with the pizza box on the coffee table in front of us, I hit PLAY.

And, as usual, I screamed at the poem at the end.

Chapter 7

One minute I was sitting on the couch with Marcie, watching *Rachel and Damien,* the next I was lying next to her and it was Saturday.

We must have fallen asleep during the movie, I thought. *No, I remember seeing the end. I screamed with excitement when Damien read his poem. That was just this last time, right?* I've seen it so many times it's hard to keep track.

I looked at the TV screen. The Blu-ray must have shut off on its own. Either that or Marcie turned everything off. The latter was more likely.

I walked over to the windows and opened the blinds, and then went to the kitchen for some breakfast.

It wasn't long after I'd started rummaging that Marcie awoke. She obviously wasn't up with the birds as usual, because of all the sunlight streaming in. I wondered if she likes to be more laid-back on weekends by not setting an alarm for herself. You'd think I'd know by now, being her roommate of nearly three years, but we had our own rooms with our own beds, so I never do know what time it is she gets up every morning. I just know it's *early.*

"Up already?" Marcie said as she came over to me.

"Good morning to you too," I said.

"I just don't remember the last time you were up before me," she said. "Or the last time I didn't have to play odds with your subconscious just to get you to open your eyes for just a mere moment out of the twenty-four hours that is a day."

"Mm-hmm," I said. "Yeah well, things change." I started cracking eggs to scramble.

"So, you're going to start getting up early every day now?"

"Are you crazy? No! I never said that." I beat the eggs with a whisk. "Besides, it's not exactly *early.*" I motioned to the living room windows.

"Whoa, we really slept in," Marcie said with surprise.

"You mean *you* really slept in," I corrected her. She gave me one of those I-knew-that looks. You know, the ones people give you when they really *don't* know, but smile to try to make it better.

After we'd eaten our scrambled eggs, we got ourselves presentable and went out into the city for the perfect Saturday.

This perfect Saturday included milkshakes of all sorts and cosmetologists to do up our hairs and nails into what we considered perfection. And guess what? It was practically effortless. The hardest part of the day was probably talking to the people who contributed to our happiness and contentment. *That's* how easy it was.

On our way back to the apartment—it wasn't far from where we'd gone, so we'd left our cars at home. Better burn off those milkshakes, right?—we passed a group of boys playing a game in parking spots along the road. As we walked by, action stopped and they all watched us.

Just as we were nearly past them, we could hear them whispering to each other. And then they started nudging each other and talking a bit louder. I caught snippets like "…you do…", "…no…", "…yeah, you…", "…no way…", "…I will…", "…no, you don't…", "…you…", "…I won't…"

Finally, one of them said loudly in our direction, "Hey!" We both stopped and turned to them. Some of the other boys started laughing. Not in an amused way, in a sort of excited way. "Are you…?" the one boy continued. "Who are you? Yeah, you."

"Um…." I looked at Marcie. She'd know what to say.

"We're just two girls," she said. "The city's full of them."

They all burst out laughing—the amused way, this time. I couldn't help smiling. Laughing's contagious.

"Come on," Marcie said to me. We proceeded to leave.

"Hey, hang on, hey," the boy said. The others started laughing again. I couldn't tell which kind it was this time.

"See you around," he finally said, and he and his laughing buddies got to talking and playing again.

"Don't socialize with random strangers," Marcie whispered to me. "Especially the young male kind."

Chapter 8

"If I shouldn't socialize with men—"

"Young men," Marcie interrupted me. We had just arrived at our apartment.

"Right, whatever," I said. "If I shouldn't socialize with *young* men, then why do you tease me about that boy in the coffee shop?"

"It's O.K. to socialize with them," Marcie said, "but you have to be careful. That bunch of boys looked girl hungry. You want to stay clear of those."

"O.K., then," I said, "but how do I know if they're girl hungry?"

She shrugged. "You just do. It's a woman's intuition."

"But, *I'm* a woman!" I said.

"Yes, but have you hung around many boys?"

"Well, no—"

"Then it just hasn't kicked in yet," she said simply. "Don't worry though. It should soon. You're twenty-three. You're in the dating age range. Just a few bad breakups and it'll be here in no time!"

"But I *have* had a bad breakup," I said desperately. Sometimes Marcie made me feel below average.

"Yeah, just one," she said. "I said a few."

I sat down at the counter. "Then, why do you direct me away from boys? I mean, I appreciate the sentiment, but I don't want to be the only woman in New York without it!" I gasped, "What if I'm the only one in the whole *world?*"

"You're not," Marcie said. "Some people never get it."

I stared at her. "But I thought you said all women have it!"

"I never said *all,*" she replied.

"Well then, how do you get it?"

"Bad breakups. That's what I said," she said.

"So what? Some women *don't* have bad breakups?"

"No, some women marry the first man they love, or are forced to marry someone. Or others," she continued, "just haven't learned the world. That can contribute to it."

"Well, how do I know if I've learned the world?" I was getting anxious.

"You are learning it," she replied, smiling. "I can tell."

"O.K....," I said. I felt kind of stupid because I didn't

know all that. *Marcie's just incredibly smart,* I told myself. *She should have a PHD or something.*

That night we went to bed in our own beds in our own rooms; not sleeping on the couch together.

After lunch the next day, Marcie went downstairs to plug her electric car in. She does it on a timely basis because she's afraid the power will drop super fast one day and she'll be stuck somewhere too far to walk back home.

She came up a few minutes later and said that for some reason the charging cord wasn't working. She had no clue what was wrong with it.

Not too long after, I decided I would watch a bit of TV. I hit the ON button a gazillion times—both on the remote and the TV itself. *That was really odd,* I thought. *I guess I won't be watching anything tonight.*

I tried to read a book for entertainment. I always have troubles with being content with a book, but tonight was a little easier—probably because it was my only source of entertainment at the time.

"It's not too dark yet," Marcie said as she entered the room, "but you're reading, so I'm going to turn on a light." She flipped the switch but nothing happened. "That's odd," she said.

"Yeah, nothing seems to be working today," I agreed.

"I wonder if the Internet's gone too." She got out her phone. "Nope. Works fine," she said. "Hang on! Look at the news!" She showed me her phone.

"The whole area is without power?" I said. "They think an animal cut it off?"

"Yeah," she said, pulling her phone back and putting it in her pocket. "They think it's the same one that's killing everyone, by the claw marks."

"That's killing everyone!" I exclaimed.

"Yeah, haven't you seen the news?" she said. "There's been a lot of attacks out in the rural areas and they can't figure out what it is. They even had a wildlife specialist come in, but even *they* couldn't identify the scratches found on the walls or anything else where the attacks have happened. Sometimes they can't even *find* the person's body. Just blood splotches here and there that can identify as a certain person's DNA."

I stared at her in shock. "Well, what happens when they run out of farmers to kill? Do they come for us?" I was hysterical.

"They don't know," Marcie said. "Hopefully they can

catch whatever it is before it gets to that point. The strangest thing is," she continued, "most of the reported attacks happened *inside* the person's house. They told everyone out there to not let any stray animals in their house, but somehow they keep getting in! Like they sneak in while the door is open for not even five seconds for someone to pass through. But the markings are so big…it must be ginormous!"

I didn't sleep well that night.

Chapter 9

Because Marcie wouldn't dare drive her car after she wasn't able to charge it at its assigned time, she took mine and I had to walk. What luck though, because today it was raining.

I didn't have a raincoat—not an official one, at least—so I just wore a cotton jacket and hoped it would keep me warm enough on my way to work.

Mr. Rockwell—one of my downstairs neighbors—wouldn't let me leave the complex until I'd put an embarrassing poncho on—it was warm, but still. I didn't want to be seen out in public with it on. He insisted though, so it seemed like I had no choice.

The wind whipped outside, and soon the top of my poncho was in my face and I could barely see a thing. I tried to pull my hood back, but the flying water prevented me from doing so. I started to grope around for a streetlight, bench, or anything else to grab on to.

I couldn't find anything!

I began to panic and picked up pace. A few bumps to the shin would be worth it just to find something and not feel totally lost anymore!

I practically started running. It wasn't long before I

ran smack into something—or someone.

"Maybeline!" a voice said. "Are you all right?" A pair of hands reached out and helped me to my feet. One of the same hands pulled the hood out of my face. The boy from the coffee shop! "Are you O.K.?" he asked again.

"Uh, yeah, I'm fine, thanks," I said. "How did you know it was me? *How do you know my name?*"

"I saw your face before you fell," he said. "And you were wearing a name tag the last time I saw you."

"Oh." That should've been obvious. "Well, while we're on the subject, I don't know *your* name. What is it?"

"Facetus." He reached down and shook my hand.

"I'm sorry, *what?*"

"My name is Facetus," he repeated.

"Fat-chat-what?"

He laughed. "No. Fuh-cha-too-suh," he said slowly.

"Can I just call you Fat-cha"—don't want to be offensive—"tulsa? Can I call you Tulsa?"

"Sure," he shrugged, "just as long as I know you're talking to me and not making fun of me or anything...."

"O.K.," I said. "See you later, Tulsa!"

"Wait," he said. "Will you be able to get to where it

is you're going on your own?"

I was about to give him a dirty look, but then I realized he was dead serious.

"Um...." I wasn't sure how to answer. The sincereness had caught me off guard.

"I mean, I could walk you to the coffee place or something...if that's where you're going, I mean—o-only if you want me to or something or—or you don't or...." He was talking very fast and out of control.

I couldn't help smiling. "That'd be nice, thank you."

He gave me an awkward smile and looked at the ground as he came over to stand next to me. As we started walking, I noticed he wasn't wearing a raincoat or anything. He didn't even have an umbrella.

"Are you cold?" I asked.

"What? No, I'm fine. I'm fine. How are you? Are you cold?"

"No," I said slowly, "but you're not wearing anything over your clothes like I am."

He looked puzzled.

"Because it's raining." I pointed to the sky.

"Oh! Oh, uh," he said, "I really don't mind the rain."

"At all?"

He paused. "No, not really."

When we reached the coffee shop, the rain was just letting up and the sun was poking out from behind the clouds.

"Do you need help with anything else?" he asked before leaving.

"No, I'm fine," I said. "Thank you for walking me here."

"No problem," he said. "Goodbye, Maybeline."

Chapter 10

Just as the lunch hour was starting, a group of noisy boys entered the shop. When they got closer, I recognized them as the boys I'd seen Saturday night. The ones Marcie had warned me to stay away from.

They came up to the counter. "Well, well, well," the one who'd spoke to us that night said, "fancy meeting you here." From the looks of it, he was the leader of their little troop.

"Uh, would you like some coffee?" I asked. I didn't know what else to say.

"Oh no. I don't drink warm things on a hot day."

"It's cold today...."

"Is that so? My mistake," he said. "It must feel warm because I'm standing next to something incredibly hot." The other boys around him snickered.

"Uh, do you want coffee or not...?" I trailed off as I realized I was the "incredibly hot" thing he was referring to.

"Sure...." He seemed a little annoyed I was ignoring his flirting.

"Well, what kind?" I asked.

The boy looked at his comrades. He turned back to

me. "Are you serious?"

"Y-yeah," I said uneasily.

He stared at me questioningly. "He'll never know," he said at last.

"I'm sorry, what?"

"You have a boyfriend, that's it."

"No…."

He cocked his head to the side. From the looks of it, no girl had ever turned him down before. Even his comrades looked surprised. "Fine, I'll leave," he said, "but I'll be back for you." He dramatically whipped around. His clan did the same and they all left.

He'd be back for me.

Like that wasn't unsettling.

Luckily, the rest of my shift didn't see any flirtatious guys.

Just before I left, I heard my phone buzz. It was from Mom.

Hi hon sorry I didnt get your text. I had to take my cell in to get it fixed will you come by later

Ok I sent back. I hoped Marcie was home with my car. She had two classes that day; one in the morning and one in the evening, so she was just going to stay the whole day at the university.

When I walked back to our apartment, it was confirmed that what I had dreaded was true.

Marcie wasn't back yet with my car.

I texted her: *Are you on your way*

A couple minutes later I got back: *Just started class*

Great. I would have to walk to Mom's house. When she wanted to see her girls, she wanted to see them. There's no way I could postpone it. Besides, she doesn't know my address and I knew she'd get lost trying to find it, so it's not like I could ask her to come here instead.

Dreaded walk to Rochester, here I come!

Chapter 11

After a few blocks, I heard a low rumbling sound behind me. A motorcycle rode up next to me. The driver cut the engine. "Maybeline!" It sounded like they'd been saying my name for a while.

"Huh? Oh, Tulsa," I said as I turned to the street.

"Where you going?" he asked me.

"My mom's house," I said. "My roommate has my car, so I have to walk."

"Oh," he said. "Does she live nearby?"

"No, she lives in Rochester."

"You're going to walk all the way to Rochester?"

"Yeah," I shrugged.

"But, you won't get there until after dark."

"Yeah." I paused to think. "Yeah, I guess that's true."

"You shouldn't be out after dark," he said.

"Why not?"

"Because that's when the attacks happen. You know, the unknown animal attacks that are all over the news."

"Oh, I didn't know that's when they happened," I said.

"Yes," he said. The sun went behind some clouds, so he took his sunglasses off and put them in his pocket. He pulled back his sleeve and looked at a watch on his wrist. "Well, you know, I got nothing going on. I could take you to Rochester if you'd like."

"Really? Thanks!" I said, stepping out into the street. "Wait," I said, climbing up behind him, "isn't it illegal to not wear a helmet on a motorcycle?"

He shrugged. "Probably. But I'm not worried about it."

"What if you get in an accident?"

He burst out laughing. "Oh, that's really funny, Maybeline! That's really funny!"

I didn't see what was funny about it.

He started the engine back up. I was really nervous because I'd never ridden on a motorcycle before, and on top of that, Tulsa didn't seem too cautious about it. I clung to his torso for dear life—probably tighter than I should have, but he didn't say anything.

We rode out of the parking lane and onto the main road. We soon reached a highway. We hadn't been riding it long when the sun poked out from behind the clouds again. Tulsa immediately reached for his sunglasses. Yep, the speed limit was 55 and he had both hands off the handlebars. I felt like I could vomit.

There was a point where we were behind a lot of traffic; and so Tulsa *crossed the median* and sped ahead of the traffic on the other side before getting back over. Thank God there weren't any cars in that lane for the moment we were in it.

I tried to block the rest of it out, but I could've sworn he'd run a few red lights without a care.

It was nearly dusk when Tulsa screeched to a halt. Finally, we're stopping at a stop sign.

"Where's your mom live?" he shouted over the roaring engine. I gave him the address and he continued down the road. Finally, we weren't going 25 miles over the speed limit.

When we reached Mom's house, Tulsa pulled in the driveway and cut the engine. I shakily loosened my grip on him and stumbled off his bike. My mom came out to greet me. She must have been watching for my arrival from the front window. She gave me a big hug. As she pulled away she took notice of Tulsa.

"Uh, hello." To me, she said, *"Who's this?"* I couldn't believe she was using her teasing tone in front of him.

"This is…Tulsa." When I'd turned around I saw he'd swung one of his legs over so they were both on the same side of the motorcycle. I couldn't imagine how on earth he was able to balance; the kickstand was still up.

"As in the city in Oklahoma?" my mom said.

"Nah, that's just what Maybes calls me," Tulsa said. I felt my face turn red. At first I thought he'd said "babes."

"Oh?" my mom said. I hoped she knew it was just an abbreviation of my name because even if we were dating, the last thing I'd want to do is talk to Mom about it. "So, what is your name?"

"Facetus," he replied.

"I beg your pardon?"

He smiled. I think it amused him that both my mom and I had problems with his name. "It's Facetus. My name."

"Oh…." My mom looked at me. "Well, that's quite… the interesting name…."

"Thank you…I think," he said. "Well, I'll see you around, Bels." He flipped his leg back over to the correct side and got the motor running.

"Goodbye," I said.

He smiled and waved before leaving.

Chapter 12

"Well now," my mom said as we sat down for dinner after I'd texted Marcie to let her know I wouldn't be home until tomorrow. "That boy was rather interesting."

"Mom," I said.

"What? I'm just saying."

"Mom, you never 'just say' anything."

"All right, you got me," she said. "I think he's cute. I mean, his name is hard to pronounce, but I think he's cute. So, tell me everything. How'd you two meet? How long have you been together? How—"

"Mom, we're not together," I said.

She gave me one of those mom-looks—you know, the ones that make you feel like they know all your secrets.

"I'm serious, we're just friends." Actually, I don't know if I'd go as far to say we're even friends. We haven't known each other that long.

"Come on, baby girl," Mom said. "There's no way you can be 'just friends' with a boy that cute."

"Really, Mom. We haven't known each other that long."

"Uh huh."

"Really. The only times I've seen him were last week at the coffee shop, this morning, and now this afternoon. Those are the only times I've seen him."

"Mm-hmm," she said. "And he just brought you here on the back of his motorcycle?"

"Well, yeah," I said. "Marcie has my car and if I walked here, I wouldn't arrive until after dark, which wouldn't be good because that's when the animal attacks happen."

"What are you talking about?" Mom said. "Maybeline, the police have no idea when they're happening. Last night they finished a twenty-four-hour stakeout without any problems. But when they went to tell the people in the houses they were watching, they found some of them dead. They haven't a clue when it happened or how the animal had gotten past them, but it did."

"That's odd," I said. "I wonder how Tulsa knew they happen then. He's the one who told me not to be out after dark because of that."

"I don't know," she replied. She lit up. "Speaking of which…." Oh no. "How is he? Is he nice? Is he romantic? Does he take you out to dinner?"

"Mom, I already told you," I said, "I've served him coffee, and the only other time I've seen him is today."

"Seen him...," she teased.

"Mom. You know what I mean," I said.

"I know, hon. I'm just teasing you," she said. "So, was it fun riding on his motorbike?"

"Oh no," I said. "Honestly, I was fearing for my life."

"I'm sure he's not that bad of a driver."

"You have no idea," I said. "You know, I've been thinking about his name lately...."

"Next to yours?"

I gave her a look.

"I'm kidding. Go on. You've been thinking about his name...."

"Yeah, I'm starting to wonder if he's not English."

"Honey, *we're* not English."

"I know. I mean English speaking. Like, he can speak English, but maybe it's not his first, you know?"

My mom thought about that.

"I mean, his name is really hard to pronounce and I feel like he has a little bit of an accent when he says it."

"I thought he had a bit of an accent in general," she said.

"Oh, did he?" I thought back to the sound of his voice.

"I mean, I could be wrong. I haven't known him as long as you have."

"Yeah, by like an hour," I said. "I haven't known him that long either." She didn't try to argue with me this time. I think it's because we were both lost in thought at that point.

Did Tulsa have an accent? It was debatable. I could always just listen extra closely the next time he talked to me. Yeah, that's what I'd do instead of stressing out about it right now.

Chapter 13

"Oh, honey, I miss you already," my mom said.

"I haven't even left yet," I said. It was the next day. I had just finished eating breakfast with Mom and I was going to leave for Buffalo. I had to get up extra early, but it was worth it to sleep in my old room again and wear pajamas I hadn't worn in ages.

"I know," she said quietly, smiling at me. "Oh have fun back in the city, baby girl." She hugged me tight. She pulled back and looked me in the eyes. "And be sure to keep me up to date on that boy of yours."

"Mom," I said, but I couldn't help laughing.

"All right, goodbye, sweetie," she said. "Is he coming back to pick you up?"

"Actually, I was going to see if Marcie could," I said. I pulled out my phone and messaged her. She said she didn't think she could and still get to her 9:00 class on time, but that she could come later. Mom recognized the look on my face.

"You can take my car if you'd like," she said.

"Oh but Mom, what will you have to drive?"

"You can bring it by this weekend with someone else to take you home. Like that boy. Or Marcie."

"Are you sure?" I asked.

"Positive," she said.

I gave her a big hug before walking out to the garage to get in her car. I also texted Marcie, telling her she wouldn't need to pick me up later.

Shortly after I left, I called the coffee shop to let Mr. Saperstien know I might be a few minutes late today. The phone rang and rang. I eventually got the answering machine and hung up. *Mr. Saperstien must not be there yet,* I thought. I didn't know what else I could do, so I just watched the time on the dash.

After the sun was a fair height in the sky, traffic started getting busier. I was more than halfway to Buffalo, but I wasn't sure if I'd make it there on time. I looked at the clock. 7:36. I could try calling again. At the next stoplight, I dialed the number and put my phone on speaker so I could set it down in the console. This time the phone on the other end of the line picked up.

"How may I help you?"

"Hey, Mr. Saperstien. It's me, Maybeline."

"Chevy? What's going on? Are you on your way?"

"Yeah, but I might be a bit late this morning. I wanted to call to let you know."

There was silence from the other end. "Uh, all right," he finally said. "Just get here as soon as you can."

"O.K., I will. Thank you, Mr. Saperstien. Bye." I waited for him to disconnect the line so I didn't have to take my eyes off the road in all this traffic. He'd taken that surprisingly well. Maybe it's because I went to all the trouble to tell him, and I *have* been somewhat of a good employee this last week, so….

When I finally arrived, it wasn't too long after 8:00. The coffee place hadn't fill up too much yet. The power hadn't been restored yet, so we still had to make the coffee by hand today.

When I served cups of coffee to a few different people at one table, I couldn't help but catch a snippet of their conversation.

"…attacks were really bad last night…."

"There were more animal attacks?" I asked without thinking. I immediately felt like an intruder on their own personal lives.

"Oh yes," one of them said. "It was really bad last night."

"Probably the worst of them…so far," another said.

"So, they've figured out that they've been

happening at night?" I couldn't resist asking.

"No, just that particular one," a third said. "They saw the owner of the house not long before dusk and found him dead around dawn, so it's evident that that particular one happened in the night."

"What made it really bad?" I was afraid to ask, but I had to know if I was going to be able to relax, knowing I would be O.K.

The four of them looked at each other. Finally, the fourth one spoke. "He was torn up much worse than the other bodies they found," she said. "But then again, who's to know if it's the worst? They haven't even found the rest of the bodies yet."

I nodded grimly. I'm guessing the fear was showing on my face because they all looked at me with concern.

"Chevy!" I heard Mr. Saperstien call. "Come on, we got more customers waiting!"

Chapter 14

I was practically worrying for the rest of my shift. I mean, I could take orders and stuff just fine, I just still had that tiny bit of fear in the back of my mind.

As I was driving home, I caught sight of Tulsa on his motorcycle in the parking lane. He was sitting on it the way he had yesterday with both his legs on one side. Unlike yesterday, however, it appeared that this time he had put the kickstand down. Sitting the same way next to him was a girl, and it looked like they were talking. She looked a little frightened. Maybe she'd been riding with him before.

As I continued on my way, I felt an odd twinge of jealousy. Why would I care if he was talking with some other girl? Why would that matter to me?

"Hey," Marcie said to me as I came in.

"Oh, hey, Bud," I said as Buddy jumped up on me. I set my stuff on the counter and went off to my room.

"Whoa, hang on," Marcie said. "No 'hello to you too' or anything? Are you feeling all right, Maybeline? Is something wrong?"

"No," I said, but the tone of my voice betrayed me.

"What is it? Come on, talk to me. There you go,"

she said as I sat down next to her on the couch. "Now, what's up?"

"Nothing," I said.

"It's obviously something."

"I'm just really worried about all the animal attacks," I said. "A group of customers today told me that last night was really bad."

"Oh yes, I read that too," she said. "But they'll catch whatever it is, Maybeline. They will."

"But what if they don't?"

"They will."

"How do you know?"

"I don't, but you have to have some faith," she said. "A little hope can go a long way."

"Yeah, but *I* could've been attacked last night, Marcie! *I* could have!"

"What do you mean? Were you out in the country?" she asked.

"No, but Tulsa said they attack at night. And since you had my car, I was going to walk—"

"Hold on. Who's Tulsa?"

"Oh, right. The boy from the coffee shop."

"That's his name? Tulsa?"

"No, but that's what I call him since his name is

really hard to pronounce."

"Oh," she said. She got excited. "So, you saw him again!"

"Yeah," I said. "He gave me a lift on his motorcy—"

"Ooh," she said.

"You wouldn't say that if you were there," I said. "Let's just say…he's a little reckless. No. He's *a hundred times* reckless."

"Like what? He rolls through stop signs?"

"Well, there was one point where he decided traffic was too much, so he crossed the median to go around them."

She stared wide eyed at me for a moment before saying, "He crossed the median? As in, he drove *against* the other traffic?"

I nodded. "Yep," I said.

"Whoa," she mumbled in disbelief. "And you *lived?*"

"I know, right!" I said.

"Thanks for the warning. Now I know never to go riding with *him.*" There was a pause. "I'm just kidding," she said. "I would *never* do that to you."

"No, it's just…." I trailed off. The conversation had reminded me of something. "I don't think I'm the only one he's been riding with…"

"Yeah," Marcie started to say.

"...in the last twenty-four hours."

"Oh," she said. I told her about how I'd seen him with that other girl. "Well, maybe he likes to give his friends lifts," she said. "Besides, you really don't *know* him. You really haven't seen him that much. I mean, I was just teasing you before."

"Yeah, I know...," I said. "He probably doesn't like me...like, *like* like me, but he goes out his way for me...."

"Yeah...," Marcie said. "Maybe he really *didn't* have anything going on and thought he'd be nice...and didn't he say they happen at night? Maybe he wanted to try to prevent another innocent human losing their life to some monster of a creature."

"Yeah...." I liked to think he'd done it because it was *me.*

"Or maybe he's gay," she said, typing something on her phone.

That statement gave me relief. "And so all of his friends would be girls," I said, "and he wouldn't feel romantic toward any of them!" This would be what I'd tell myself.

"Exactly," she said, still messing with her phone.

"What are you doing?" I asked her.

"Looking for something on them happening at night," she said. "I've been keeping up on the news and they haven't said anything about that." After a moment, she said, "I don't know. I can't find anything on that."

"That's odd," I said. "I wonder how Tulsa knows."

"Maybe he's a police officer and they just haven't announced their theory yet until they're more certain," she shrugged.

"Maybe…," I said. "No, with his driving skills, I can't imagine how that'd even be a job *option.*"

"That's true…," she said. "Oh well. Maybe he just heard it from somebody else who was wrong, or maybe he misunderstood them or something, I don't know," she shrugged again.

"Yeah." I believed that. After all, hadn't Mom and I concluded English wasn't his first language? My thoughts were satisfied for the rest of the night.

Chapter 15

I didn't see Tulsa at all for the next couple of days. Either it seemed like he was everywhere or he had vanished. I also didn't see that group of boys either to my relief.

I must have jinxed it though, because just as I was beginning to think their leader had forgotten about me during the afternoon on Friday, he and his clan entered the shop.

"So shocked to see me?" he said. "Told you I'd be back. Now, I want you as my date. Now, normally I'd choose the day, but seeing you're such a pennant woman, I—"

"Independent," one of the other boys whispered to him.

"You were supposed to say 'independent,'" another said.

"What?" he said to them. "Is that even a real thing?"

They all said yes and nodded in agreement.

"Remember, we rehearsed it that way," a third said.

The rest of them showed their agreement.

"Well, maybe I need to write the lines next time," he said with the authority of a leader. "Something that actually makes sense!"

"Oh, but women love being called independent," a fourth said. "It really flatters them!" The rest of them joined in, trying to convince him.

"Um, excuse me," a familiar voice said, "are you in line for something?"

"Oh no. Go ahead," one of the boys from the group said. "We're just having a discussion about something."

"Oh, all right," Tulsa said. He turned to me. "Hey," he greeted me.

"Hey." I couldn't help smiling at the sight of him.

"Could you make me another cappuccino… please?" he added.

"Yeah," I said. "To go or stay?"

"To go," he said.

"O.K.," I said. "Guess what, they fixed the power, so we get to use the machines again!" I told him as I made up his order.

"That's great!" he said, smiling. He had a beautiful smile.

"Yeah." I finished stirring it up and handed it to him.

The clan had stopped arguing at this point and their leader looked mad that I had given all my attention to

Tulsa.

"Thank you, Maybeline," he said, still smiling.

"Thank you." I smiled back at him.

"No, I'm thanking you," he laughed, his amber eyes dancing.

"What?"

He laughed again. "I'm thanking you for making me coffee."

"Oh." I set my elbows on the counter and put my chin in my hand.

"And here's the money for it," he said, pulling it from his pocket with his free hand and holding it out.

"O.K.," I said.

"I'll just set it on the counter," he said after a brief pause.

"Yeah," I said. "Oh!" I stood upright. "Oh, I'm—I'm supposed to take that."

"Yeah...," he said. At least he was still smiling, so I didn't feel like a complete moron. I put the money in the cash register, trusting it was the right amount.

"I'm going to go now," he said, "O.K.?"

"O.K.," I said.

"Bye, Maybes." He waved and left.

"Bye," I said.

Someone cleared his throat.

"Oh, *you're* still here," I said, hoping my annoyance was obvious. His annoyance was obvious too.

"Come on," one of his members said. "We can go home and rehearse something else."

He glared at him. He turned his unwelcoming stare to me like he was going to say something, but instead turned around and stomped out the door. His troop looked at me, then followed their master out.

Chapter 16

Out the window next to an empty booth, I could clearly see Tulsa. It looked like he was talking to that girl I'd seen him with on Tuesday. I couldn't tell what they were saying though. I didn't recognize the movements of their lips. I didn't get to watch long though, because there were more customers coming up to the counter and I needed to take their orders.

When I did look back at the window, they weren't talking anymore. They were still there, but they were definitely, certainly, *undeniably* not talking….

I slammed the door shut. "You lied to me!" I said.
"About what?" Marcie asked.
"Tulsa," I said, setting my stuff down and rummaging through the fridge. "You told me…that he…"—I found what I was looking for—"was gay!" I slammed the door shut and reached up into the cupboard.
"I said *maybe*. I never said he actually was," she answered.
"Still!" I set the box of crackers on the counter and started spraying whipped cream on them as I took

them out. "I had it in my head, and guess what!"

"You're getting whipped cream all over the counter," she said. I glared at her. "Which, isn't important," she said. "Why? How do you know?"

"You know how I said I saw him with another girl?" I said, beginning to eat the whipped cream-covered crackers.

"Yeah?"

"Well, I thaw 'im wibber again!" I said, my mouth full.

"So?" she said.

"So!" I spread another cracker. "He was with her! Like, *with* her!"

Marcie looked confused, so I continued. "First they were talking"—I chewed the cracker and swallowed—"and then they were…they were…!"

"What?"

"Kissing!" I let my head fall in my folded arms on the countertop. Marcie was silent. I sat down in one of the stools and lifted my head. "And just earlier," I said calmer, "he was in the shop…and he was laughing and smiling at me and I—" *And I what?* I thought to myself. *I…thought he liked me…even though I thought he was gay? What is wrong with me? How can that work?*

"Maybe he thinks you're funny," she said. Of course. He thinks I'm a hysterical goof. *Of course.* "In a good way," she added quickly, reading my face. "Maybe you brighten up his morning."

"Maybe," I grumbled.

"But maybe...," she said, "maybe you could get him to come over sometime...or something." I knew she didn't want to say it, but she wanted to check him out. I *knew* it.

"Great," I said aloud. "Now I have *two* girl-hungry boys bothering me."

"Two?" Marcie said. I nodded and told her about the boy we'd seen the last weekend. "And he just keeps coming back?" she said. "That doesn't sound good. I'm sorry you have to deal with that, Maybeline."

"Yeah," I shrugged.

"Aw, Buddy can tell you're in distress," she said as Buddy put his front paws up on the stool and started licking me.

"Thank you, Bud," I said, petting him. "So, the next time I see Tulsa I need to invite him over?"

"Well, I mean, you don't *have to,"* Marcie said, but I could tell she wanted me to.

Chapter 17

The next time I saw Tulsa was Sunday morning.

I had just come back from dropping my mom's car off at her house. Marcie had gone with me in my car, and on the way home she sat in the passenger seat while I drove. I had dropped her off at our apartment door and I had just finished parking my car in our garage. I saw him on the sidewalk as I was walking around the building. "Hey, Tulsa!" I said.

He stopped. "Hi, Maybeline."

"Do you want to come have brunch with me and my roommate?"

"I'm sorry, what?"

"Brunch. Do you want to come have brunch with me and my roommate?"

He stared at me for a moment. "What is that?" he asked.

"It's like breakfast and lunch," I said.

"Those are the same thing? I thought they were different."

"No, they are different," I said. "Brunch is a meal you eat *in between* breakfast and lunch. Well, actually, you don't usually eat breakfast or lunch on days you have brunch—" He looked confused, so I just summed it up. "It's when you eat a big breakfast instead of having lunch," I said.

"Oh, O.K." He still seemed a little confused, but I think it made more sense now.

"So, do you want to come have brunch with us?" I asked.

He looked at his watch. "How long will that take?"

"Um, not long," I said. "Do—do you have something else going on?"

"Oh no. No, I can come do…that with you."

"O.K.," I said. "Our apartment's up here." I led him to the door of the complex.

"What do you eat for brunch?" he asked as we walked up the stairs.

"Anything we want, I guess," I said. "My roommate's making it right now. We're probably going to have bacon or waffles or something."

"Hey, by the way," I said as we reached my apartment. I paused on purpose so I could hear his voice again.

"What?" he asked. Mom was right. He did have a slight accent, it just wasn't very obvious.

"Do you speak English?" I asked.

"Yes." He gave me a look. "Yes, I speak English. Do *you* speak English?"

"No, I mean, are you—like, are you American?"

"Yes, I'm American," he said.

"No, I mean, like…." I thought about it. "Is English a language you speak? Like, normally? Like, something you always speak?" I was having a hard time figuring out how to ask this question.

He thought for a moment. "You mean, do I speak more than one language?"

"Yeah!" I said. "Well, no." He stared at me. "Like, is English your first language? Like, the first language you learned? Like, as a baby you learned it listening to your parents or did they speak another language and you learned it in a class in school or something?"

"No," he said. "No, I didn't learn…what my parents spoke…in school."

"No, I mean English," I said. "Did you learn English in school? Like, you spoke another language before you spoke English?"

"Yes," he said slowly, thinking. "Yes, I learned English in school when I was a kid. Why do you ask? Do I speak English bad?"

"Oh no," I said, "you speak English fine. In fact, you

speak it really good. I wouldn't have known it was your second language. I was just curious."

"Do you speak English?" he asked me.

"Oh no. No, that's not how you ask," I said. "I just didn't know...how to ask." I smiled sheepishly.

"Do you speak another language?"

"Yes! Yes, there it is! Yes, that's how you ask!" I said, pointing at him and jumping up and down. "Um, no," I said, calming down. "English is all I've spoken my entire life." I'd never felt too bad about it before, but I suddenly felt embarrassed I hadn't ever taken the time to learn another way of communicating. "So, what's your first language?" I asked. "Like, the one your family speaks?"

"Hmm...," he said. "I don't know how to say it in your language."

"O.K.," I said. And it was. I didn't really need to know.

Chapter 18

The apartment door swung open. "Oh, hey, Maybeline," Marcie said, "you're bac—*hello.*" She turned to Tulsa. "Are you from the coffee shop?" she asked him.

"Um, no?" Tulsa said.

"Yes," I said. I said to him, "She was asking if you were the person I told her about that I met in the coffee shop."

"Oh…." He looked at Marcie. He had that didn't-know-I-was-being-discussed look.

"Come in," Marcie said. "I'll be back in a minute." She turned and went down our apartment hall.

"Well, it looks like we're having bacon, eggs, and waffles," I said as we came inside. "Hey, do you think I'm funny?" It felt like a weird question to ask, but since Marcie wasn't here and I was already learning stuff from him, I really wanted to ask.

"Yes," he said. "Yes, you make me laugh."

"Like, in a bad way?"

"No, why would that be bad?"

"Well, I mean, you don't think I'm silly, do you? Like—like a child?"

"But, you are a child," he said.

"I'm twenty-three!" I couldn't believe what I was hearing.

"Maybe 'child' means something different to you than it does to me," he said.

"What does 'child' mean to you?" I asked.

"A child is a person with a young mind," he answered. "It doesn't matter how old they are, just that they're creative, adventurous, fun…innocent."

"Are you a child?" I asked. Under his philosophy, I actually *liked* being called a child. In fact, I think I'd be sad if I wasn't.

"Oh, no," he said. "No, I'm not, no."

"Do you wish you were?"

"I couldn't," he said. "No, that wouldn't be good if I was."

"Why not?" I couldn't see what was wrong with being creative or adventurous.

"Because I have to—I just can't because of…"—he looked at the ground—"things that…happen."

I was about to ask what, but at that moment Marcie came back from her bedroom. "O.K., I'm back," she said. She had a notepad in one hand and a pencil in the other.

"You're going to interrogate him?" I knew Marcie meant well, but this was a little much.

She held up a finger for me to be quiet.

"So…." Marcie looked at Tulsa, pencil in position. "What's your name?" she asked.

"Facetus," he answered.

"What?" she said, staring at him.

I could see why Tulsa found it amusing when people had troubles with his name—because it was!

"Hey, look who's up from his nap!" I said as Buddy came out into the kitchen. He stopped dead in his tracks. Then he started barking and growling ferociously.

"Whoa!" I said, grabbing on to his collar just before he lunged for Tulsa. "Calm down, boy! Calm down!" It was taking a lot of effort to keep him back. "I'm sorry. He's not usually like this," I said to Tulsa.

"It's all right," he said. "Dogs usually don't like me."

"Yeah, but, I don't think Buddy's ever *not* liked anybody," I said, looking at the golden retriever. "I've never seen him do this before."

"You know, they say dogs can sense things," Marcie whispered to me.

Chapter 19

I had to shut Buddy in my room for brunch. Marcie and I had a little bit of everything. I don't think Tulsa had any of the eggs or waffles—or at least, I didn't see him eat any. He just piled his plate full of bacon and ate that while Marcie flooded him with questions.

"Name?"

"Facetus."

"Age?"

"Um...."

"How old are you?" I helped him.

"That"—he paused to chew—"would be older than you."

"How much older?" Marcie watched him with scrutinizing eyes.

"Not a lot."

I could tell Marcie wasn't completely satisfied, but she continued on to the next question.

"Dating status?"

"Dating what?"

"Like, are you dating anybody right now or are you single?"

"No, I'm not dating anyone," he said. "I don't know

what the last part meant."

"Single means you're not dating anyone," I said. He nodded.

"How many exes do you have?" she asked. This was getting very awkward and embarrassing for me, so I could only imagine how awful it must have been for Tulsa.

"X's?" he asked. "None. My name is F-A-C-E-T-U-S. There are no x's."

"Exes as in girlfriends," Marcie said slowly, giving him a strange look.

"I don't have any…girlfriends," he said. "Girls you date or friends?"

"Date."

"None."

"Ex-girlfriends," I said. "Girls you used to date but don't anymore."

"Right. None," he said.

What?

"You're telling me you've never dated a girl before?" Marcie said.

"No," he said.

"Have you dated *anyone*?"

"No."

Marcie opened her mouth to speak. I could tell she was about to blurt out something like *What is wrong with you?* but she caught herself.

"Do you like Maybeline?" she said.

He smiled. "Of course I do," he said. "I love her."

Chapter 20

There was an awkward silence.

Marcie couldn't hold herself back this time. "All right!" she said, standing up. "All right! I've had enough of these games! I want to know the truth!"

Tulsa stared at her. "The—the truth?"

"Yes! *The truth,*" Marcie said. "How old are you exactly, are you dating anyone, are you not dating anyone, *have* you dated people before and *how many?* And last, but certainly not least, do you really love Maybeline, or is it just some sort of act you're putting on, like *Ooh, look at me, I'm helping Maybeline* and *Ooh, look at me, I'm really nice and I—*"

Tulsa slowly turned to me with shock evident on his face as Marcie continued her outburst.

"—and *why* did you try to kill her?" Marcie finally ran out of breath and stopped.

"Excuse me," Tulsa said, *"kill her?"*

"Yeah," Marcie said. "Stop playing all innocent. You had her get on the back of your stupid motorcycle and you took her on the other side of the median! She could have died!"

"No, she wouldn't," he said.

"Yeah, she would!"

"No, most of the cars in front of us were going fifty-three point two eight miles per hour," he said. "Three of them were going fifty-two point seven, four of them fifty-three point four, and seven of them fifty-one point nine. The cars on the other side of the median going the opposite way were going an average of fifty-seven point six, and at the time I crossed, the car in front on the inside lane was two point seven miles away from us, and the next break in the median was one point two miles away. After I crossed the median, I accelerated to about ninety-four point six eight miles per hour and got to the next opening, still being a safe enough distance away from on-coming traffic while surpassing the traffic traveling in the same direction. Maybeline was perfectly safe. I would never purposely put her in any direct danger."

Neither Marcie nor I knew what to say.

"My god," I said at last, "you're a genius!"

"O.K.....". He didn't seem to really understand.

"It means you're really smart," I told him.

"I know," he said. "Thank you."

"Yeah well, *you're not off the hook!*" Marcie said, having found her voice again. "If you really loved

Maybeline, then why were you kissing that other girl just outside the coffee shop!"

Marcie went too far.

I know it's pathetic, but I covered my eyes with my hands. I thought at the time it'd be better than watching this go down.

"What?" I heard Tulsa say eventually.

"Yeah," she said. "Maybeline told me all about it!"

I slowly removed my hands to see Tulsa looking at me. He didn't say anything for a moment, looking back and forth between Marcie and me. Finally, he stood up and said, "If you brought me here so you could yell at me, I'm leaving!"

"Wait, no"—I grabbed his arm as he passed me—"Tulsa, that's not what I—that's not why I—"

"Is it?" His black eyes stared into mine.

"No, I—" Wait. *Black* eyes? "What happened to your eyes? I thought they were golden. Now they're black."

He looked down and blinked a few times before putting his sunglasses on…inside.

He took a deep breath. "What is it you want to tell me, Maybeline?" His voice sounded different…but I couldn't place it. Was it lower in pitch or was it just because he was upset or was it merely my imagination?

"I...." I'd forgotten. I couldn't help but notice his veins stuck out of his neck like he was squeezing his muscles as hard as he could or refraining from coughing or something. "Are you O.K.?"

"Yes, I—"

"I don't have time for this!" Marcie said. I turned around and made gestures telling her I wanted her to be quiet. She didn't get the message. "Do you *really* love Maybeline? *Yes* or *no?*"

"Yes, of course," he said. "She's my friend." He looked at me. "Right?"

"Right," I said, smiling. I was *his friend.*

"Um...," Marcie said. "You mean you *like* her?"

He stared at her. "Is it 'like'? I thought it was 'love.' Oh, I'm always getting those two mixed up!" He laughed and removed his sunglasses.

His eyes were their normal color again.

Chapter 21

The rest of Tulsa was relaxed again as he laughed.
"Oh, what did I say?" he said.

"You said you…loved her." I could tell Marcie was confused. At least she wasn't yelling anymore.

"You say 'love' to people you love…like date. You say 'I love you' to people you date and people you marry, and you say 'I like you' to your friends," I explained.

"Oh," Tulsa said, smiling. I was proud of myself for coming up with a good explanation. "So, I like you?" he said, motioning to me.

"Right," I said. "I like you too, by the way." I smiled. He smiled brighter.

Marcie was still confused. "You get 'love' and 'like' mixed up?"

"He doesn't speak English," I told her.

"I speak English," he said.

"Well yeah, obviously," I said. "It's just not your first."

"Yes," he said, "but I still speak it."

"Hold on, English is your second language?" Marcie said. "Oh that makes so much more sense now!"

"She doesn't mean it in a bad way," I quickly told Tulsa. "She doesn't mean it obvious because you're not good at it or anything, she means it because you… had a few more questions than most English speakers would have. Like, *native* English speakers."

"Kind of like Maybeline," Marcie teased me. "You don't know it as well as people who have always spoken it," she said to Tulsa.

"I thought Maybeline's always spoken English," he said.

"Oh, she has," Marcie said. "That's the joke."

"Like I can't speak it as well," I explained, even though I wasn't too thrilled about Marcie's joke. "Like, I'm a social outcast or something." I paused. "Nothing bad to you, just that it's something I've always speaken and—"

"Spoken," Marcie said.

It took me a moment to understand. When I did, I glared at her.

After a few more embarrassing moments for me, Tulsa said he was going to go. Just as he was closing the door behind him, I quickly jumped up, saying, "Wait!" and opened the door to go out into the hallway with him. I closed the door behind me and said, "Could you teach me how to say your name? Like, your *actual* name?"

He smiled. "Sure. You say 'fuh.'"

"Fuh," I repeated.

"Cha."

"Cha."

"Toos."

"Toos," I said.

"Fuh…cha…toos," he said.

"Fuh…cha…toos," I said. "Fuh-chat-toos. Fuh-chat-toos. Facetus."

"Yes, that's right!" he said.

"Yay, I can say your name!" It felt a little weird to say something like that, but hey, *I can say his name!*

"Good job," he laughed.

"Yeah," I said. "Glad I accomplished something," I laughed.

"Thank you for taking the time to do that," he said.

"Well yeah," I said, "I mean, *you* know a whole other language, I mean…learning your name is really the least I can do, right?"

"Still," he said, "not everyone would have taken the time to do that." I shrugged. "Thank you, Maybeline. I lov—like you." We both laughed. "I'll work on it," he said.

"O.K.," I said. "Bye…Facetus."

"Bye." His hand went up behind my head and he pulled my face close to his so that our mouths touched before turning and going down the complex stairs.

Chapter 22

 I stumbled through the door.

 Marcie was sitting at the counter, going through her notes again, like she was trying to re-evaluate Facetus.

 Should I say it? Or should I not? I wanted someone to talk to about it, but I wasn't sure if Marcie was up for that right now.

 "M-Marcie," I tested the waters.

 "What?" she said, still looking at her notepad.

 "Could I…talk to you…about something?"

 "Sure."

 "Like, something serious with your undivided attention?"

 She put her pad down and swirled around in her stool to face me. I sat down across from her.

 "Facetus…," I began. She stared at me. "The boy who was just here," I clarified. She nodded. "He, um… he, uh…."

 "What?" she asked.

 "He just—he just kissed…me." Marcie's jaw dropped. "But it wasn't like any kiss I'd had before," I said. "There was something different about…."

"What?" I was glad Marcie was still with me.

"I don't know, it just…felt different."

"Like, how would you describe it?"

"I can't. I don't know how to put it in words…."

"Was it just a light peck, or was it like *I want you*?"

"No, it was pretty quick, just brief," I said.

"Was it on the cheek? I read that in some cultures, that's a sort of greeting."

"No, it was on the lips," I said.

"Gee…," she said. "I don't know, Maybeline. I'm going to be honest with you about something though. He's weird, and I don't like him."

I smiled. Gotta love Marcie and her honesty.

When I went down the hall to my bedroom, I was greeted by Buddy.

"Hey, Bud," I said. He quickly scampered out of the room and was all business. Sniff-sniff here and sniff-sniff there. When he was finally satisfied that he found no Facetus here, he ran back to me.

I dropped to my knees with outstretched arms to greet him.

He came over and showered me with canine love.

Tail a-waggin', ears a-floppin', and tongue a-lickin', yep…it was great to be a dog owner. How they're always so excited to see you and—

"Oh my god!" I said suddenly. "Oh my god, Marcie! Oh my god! I know now! Oh my god!"

"What? What is it?" Marcie asked.

"Oh my god, I know now!" I stood up and walked over to her. "I know!"

"You know what?" she asked.

"Facetus's kiss! I know how to describe it!"

"Well?"

"It's like a doggie kiss!"

Marcie gave me a look. "He licked you? Oh why I—"

"No, Marcie," I laughed. "I meant the feeling. Like, you know you're appreciated, but it's very simple and not romantic by any means. *That's* what his kiss was like!"

"Wow, I don't think I've ever had that before...," she said.

"Yeah, me neither," I said. "Well, except for Buddy." I looked down. He was smiling with his tongue hanging out—imagine if he knew he was the reason for our victory!

<u>Chapter 23</u>

When I went downstairs for work the next morning, I got pointed at by Mr. Rockwell.

"That girl right there!"

"I don't see no girl!" my other elderly downstairs neighbor, Ms. Fellers, said.

"She's right there! She came down the stairs!"

"I think you're starting to see things, Frank!"

"No, no. Your glasses are broken!"

"My glasses work fine!"

"If they worked fine, you done have seen her!"

"You don't want to get in a fight with me, laddie!"

"I'm telling you. And she had some boy with her yesterday! He was up in her apartment for four hours! That's far too long for young people these days!"

"It was twenty minutes," I told him.

"What'd you say, you darn talking coatrack!" Ms. Fellers yelled at me.

"The thingamabob was at the twelve when he came, and when he left it was at the four!" Mr. Rockwell said.

"Was it the long thingamabob or the short thingamabob?" I asked calmly. You have to be extra nice to the elderly.

"The one that moves," Mr. Rockwell said. "The tiny one ain't move no more!"

"That would be the minute hand, Mr. Rockwell," I said before leaving. I could still hear him and Ms. Fellers arguing as I left.

When I started walking down the steps, I caught sight of Facetus. He was standing on the sidewalk with the other girl.

Wasn't that the shirt he was wearing yesterday? I thought. *Oh well.* "Hey!" I said.

When the girl turned to look at me with her frightened eyes, she quickly clung to Facetus and hid behind him. He turned to look at her and spoke to her quietly. When he turned to me, who by then had reached the sidewalk, she still remained in her position. I wondered what he had said to her.

"Hi, Maybeline," he said.

"Hi," I said. "Is she all right?"

"Oh she's—don't worry about her. She's just a little shy, that's all." He turned to her again and mumbled something else. Eventually she dropped her lock on his torso and he stepped aside so I could see her. I wondered if she was a "child" too. Facetus had an arm over her shoulder. By how timid she seemed, I bet it was to make her feel better…yes, that's what I'd tell myself….

"Hi." I waved to her. She tried to shimmy back to her hiding place.

"No no, it's O.K.," Facetus said, not letting her hide again. He pointed to me. "Maybeline. May-bel-ine. Maybeline," he said to her.

"Nay-nel-ine," she mumbled, her blue eyes wide, watching me carefully…in fear it seemed. By the way she pronounced my name and how Facetus had slowed it down for her, I wondered if she didn't speak much English like he did.

Maybe she was one of his family members and I just misinterpreted what I saw out the coffee shop window, I thought.

"It's nice to meet you," I said in a slower voice than I normally would. She looked at Facetus. He gestured toward me, and with his hands on her shoulders moved her closer to me so we were face to face. "I'm Maybeline," I continued. "What's your name?"

She stared blankly at me.

"You remember your name," Facetus said. It wasn't a question, it was an encouragement.

"H-Hazy," she said.

"Haz*ley,*" he said.

"Haz…*ley,*" she repeated.

"Yes," he said. "Hazley," he said in an addressing tone. She turned to him. "Maybeline"—he walked over to me—"is an angel." And with that, he kissed me on the cheek.

"Maybeline…is an angel," she repeated. It wasn't said in any emotion, it was just simply stated. I wasn't sure, but I thought I saw a slight smile on her lips as she looked at me now.

"You think I'm an angel?" I turned my head to look at Facetus. I don't think I'd ever smiled brighter in my life. That was quite the compliment I'd never gotten before! I didn't even care I sounded like a chipmunk now.

"Well yeah," he said. "You're so sweet and nice." I could melt into him right now.

"Maybeline," Hazley said. I looked at her. "Facetus love you, I love you," she said.

I reached over and hugged her. She was warm. I noticed her arms didn't wrap around me. I stepped back and looked at her. She looked confused, like she didn't understand what I was doing.

"Do you not do that in your culture?" I asked Facetus.

"What?" he asked.

"Hugging. Do you not really do that where you're from or with your family? Is that not something you do?"

"No, not really," he answered. "I mean, we do *sometimes,* but it's not really common."

"Well, how do you show your friends and family members you appreciate them? That's what we do. We hug. What do you do?"

"Um, that's a bit hard to answer," he said. "It depends on who you talk to about it because it's different for different people. Um, if you're asking me specifically, I kiss my friends."

"Oh." There's another question cleared up. "Is that just something you do, or is that something other people do?"

"Eh," he said, "some do, some don't."

Chapter 24

"Do you not have work today?" Facetus asked, looking at his watch.

"No, I do," I said. "Why?"

"I just assumed it opened at eight," he said.

"Yeah, it does...."

"Well, it's seven fifty-seven right now—"

"Holy crap!" I said and turned, running to the parking area around the building. "Bye!" I called over my shoulder and waved.

"Oh no oh no oh no," I said as I got in the car. I could've just asked Facetus if he'd take me on his motorcycle, but I didn't think I was up for that kind of adventure this morning—even if he was a true genius!

I zipped out of the parking lot and tried to get there as soon as possible! No such luck. I was caught in the morning traffic and didn't get there as quickly as I'd wanted to.

"I am *so* sorry, Mr. Saperstien," I said as I rushed in.

"Chevy, are you kidding me?" he said.

"I know I know I know," I said, hurrying into my name tag and apron.

"So…Chevy. That's your name." Uh oh.

"Excuse me…um, what's your name?" I asked the clan leader.

"Robert."

"Excuse me, Robert," I said, "but I have work to do, so unless you want coffee—"

"All right, Friday it is," he said. "I'll be here to pick you up." His group started laughing and high-fiving him, saying things like "good one" and "oh yeah" as they left with him.

The next day, Facetus came into the coffee shop with Hazley, guiding her by the hand. She seemed a little frightened, but once her eyes found me, she relaxed a bit.

"Did you like the coffee you tried last time?" he asked her as they reached the counter. When she didn't answer, he started whispering in her ear with mouth movements I didn't recognize. I wondered why he couldn't speak in his native language at a regular volume. When he stepped away from her ear, she nodded.

"O.K.," he said. "We'll have two cappuccinos please, Miss Maybeline."

"O.K." I smiled. Hearing his cheerful voice always made my whole day a little better. "Here. To go, I assu—Hey, what happened to your hand?" I'd given Hazley her cup but paused on Facetus's as I looked at his outstretched hand. There were a bunch of tiny narrow cuts across his palm. He looked down at it, as if he didn't know there was anything wrong.

"Oh, it—it's nothing," he said, hastily putting it in his pocket. Hazley was watching him closely now with fear. Why did that girl always look scared? "Here." He handed me money for both the drinks in his opposite hand and took his drink from me in the same one. "Good day, Maybeline. Come on, Hazley," he said in monotone as he left with Hazley close behind.

That was odd.

The rest of my shift went well—no sign of Robert and his clan. When I got home, however, Marcie seemed anxious.

"Maybeline!" she said.

"What?"

"O.K., I know I said not to worry about the animal attacks, but I was just watching the news—"

"What? What happened?" I set my stuff down and went in the living room to sit with her on the couch.

"They found the blood of the animal—"

"What? How did that happen? Does that mean it's dead and won't attack anymore?"

"No," she said. "In an attack last night, it broke a decoration or something in the person's house, and they found its blood on some of the broken pieces."

"And?"

"And they had it examined by scientists so they would know what kind of animal it is, and…and…!"

"What?"

"They don't know what kind of animal it is!" she said.

"But I thought you said they looked at it—"

"It's nothing they've ever seen before," she said. "It's a creature society doesn't even *know about* yet! No wonder we haven't caught it yet! And it's just going to keep killing and killing and kil—and—" She started crying. I hugged her. If Marcie was worried, then the whole world should be.

This is really, really bad.

Chapter 25

I didn't see Robert and his clan Wednesday and Thursday. I also didn't see Facetus to my disappointment. When Friday rolled around, however, Robert arrived just at the end of my shift to pick me up for the date he'd promised me on Monday.

"So…Chevy," he said. It was odd to see him without his troop.

"Actually, it's Maybeline," I said.

"Right…Maybeline," he said. He extended his elbow. "Shall we?"

"Look, Robert, you're really nice and all, it's just—"

"You're going to go back on your promise?"

"I never promised anything."

"Oh that's such a shame," he said. "'Cause I'm taking you anyway."

I rolled my eyes. "Well, I've got to finish cleaning up before I'm going *anywhere."*

"I'll wait," he said.

"Ugh!" I overemphasized my annoyance. I tried to slack as much as I could, but I eventually ran out of tasks and didn't know what else to do. *Well, girl-hungry boys tend to be flaky, right?* I thought. *I'll go on*

this one date with him and he'll stop bothering me. "All right," I said at last with a sigh. "Let's go." As I walked out the door with Robert, I quickly messaged Marcie I'd be home later on.

When I got in his car, he immediately sped off toward the highway. After some time, we arrived at a fancy restaurant and he treated me to dinner. I tried to hurry, but he seemed to try to make the night as long as possible.

At the end of supper, we went out to his car and he was going to drive me home. I started to relax—until I realized I didn't know where we were.

"Where are we going?" I asked. "Where are we going? I want to know! I need to get home!"

"Oh relax," he said. "We're just going to my place."

"'We'?"

"Come on, it'll be fun."

"No, it won't. I want to go home," I said sternly.

"Chill, we're almost there," he said.

"No! I don't want to go to your house!" Screw his feelings. "I didn't even want to go to dinner with you tonight! So let me go home!"

"See? It wasn't that far, was it?" he said, ignoring me as he parked in front of a house. He got out of the car then walked around to open my door.

"Look," I said as the passenger door was shut, "I don't know wha—" But I didn't get to finish that statement because he pressed me against the car door and started to kiss me. "Stop!" I turned my head away from him.

"Come on, it'll be fun," he said, positioning my face back to his with his hands.

"No, stop!" I tried to pull him back from me. His hands tried to make their way under my shirt. "No, I don't want to have sex with you!"

Just then a light came on. *Saved by the bell.* "What's going on out there?" I heard a cranky voice screech.

Robert took a step back as he turned to the distant porch light. "Nothing, Mrs. Papagratis."

I took that opportunity and ran.

As I raced down the sidewalk, I pulled my phone out of my pocket and dialed Marcie's number.

Chapter 26

"This is why I look out for you, Maybeline," Marcie said. "I don't mean to be annoying, I just hate to see things like this happen."

It was early Saturday morning. I'd spent all night on the couch with Marcie, listening to her talk as if I hadn't been stupid by not heeding her warning.

"I'm so sorry, Marcie," I said.

"Why are you sorry? You're the one who's hurt." She had me in a sisterly hug. "We can report it."

"But nothing actually happened. His neighbor came out and I was fine."

"Still," she said.

There was a knock at the door.

"Whoever it is, tell them to go away," I said, burying my face in the seat cushions as she got up.

"Hello!" I heard a cheerful voice say as Marcie opened the door.

"Maybeline's not feeling well right now," I heard Marcie say.

"Oh, that's too bad," Facetus said. "Is it just a cold?"

"I'm not contagious!" I quickly shouted.

"Well, I guess a visitor or two is fine," Marcie said.

"Hey, Maybeline," Facetus said in a soft, sympathetic tone. I lifted my face out of the cushions and sat up. He sat down next to me. "I'm sorry to hear you're not feeling well," he said.

"Thanks," I said. "You're not afraid of catching my cold?"

"Well, you said you weren't contagious, didn't you?" He smiled. I smiled back.

"We find something we think you like!"

I looked up and saw Hazley was here too. She handed me something shiny. "It's beautiful!" I said, looking at the horse trinket on the silver chain. "Is this real silver?"

"Um, I don't know," Facetus said. "Does it look real to you?"

"It doesn't matter," I said. "I was just curious. Did you know that I loved horses growing up?"

"I did not," he said. "That worked out perfectly, didn't it?"

"Yeah, it did," I said. "Where did you find it?"

"Oh, just…around." Facetus scratched the back of his neck.

"It's absolutely beautiful," I said, taking one last look

at the galloping horse. "Thank you." I looked him in those beautiful eyes of his. He smiled. "Will you put it on me?"

"Sure," he said. I rotated my body so my feet were facing the arm of the couch and my back was facing him. He put the chain around my neck slowly and carefully as if he was afraid he'd hurt me at the touch of his fingers.

"Thank you." I turned back around to face him, fingering the still figure that rested on my chest. "I love it!"

"I'm glad you do," he said. "Wait, doesn't that mean you want to marry it or something?"

"No, that's people," I said. "It's different with objects."

He slowly nodded.

"How are you feeling, Maybeline?" Marcie asked me.

"Much better," I told her.

"Do you know what you have?" Facetus asked me.

"Oh no, I'm not sick," I said. "I just didn't want to see anybody today." He paused. "But you're not anybody," I added, "you're a friend!"

He smiled slightly. "Why don't you want to see

anybody?"

"I'm just not feeling well enough to," I said. "I mean, I'm not sick or anything…I'm just not feeling up to it because of something that happened…last night…."

"What? What happened last night?" He seemed deeply concerned.

"Uh, it's nothing…," I said. "It's just…I went out with someone…and it just…didn't go how I wanted it to."

"Oh?"

"Yeah," I said. "You shouldn't worry about it. I probably overreacted."

"No you didn't!" Marcie said. "That was a sick thing for him to pull!"

"What? What did he do?" Facetus asked. Hazley was looking at me too. I wondered how much of this she could understand.

"Nothing, just…." I didn't know what I was going to tell him. "He, um, he…tried to do something to me…I didn't want him to…."

"What?"

"Um…." I looked at Marcie. I knew she normally wouldn't say anything since it's not her thing to tell, but when I gave her that look, she would know I needed her to.

"He sexually assaulted her," Marcie plainly said.

"Well, he didn't actually. His neighbor came out and —"

"Yes, he still did!" Marcie said. "It doesn't matter if he finished."

"He did that to you?" Facetus used that different tone in his voice I'd heard on Sunday. "Did you tell him to stop?"

"Yeah, from the beginning, I was screaming at him —"

"I will tear him apart!"

Chapter 27

We all stared at Facetus.

"You'll do *what?*" I said.

"No no, Facetus," Hazley said. "No…."

"I will," Facetus said. "You don't deserve to be treated like that and he needs to know that!" I could see his pupils getting incredibly large. Was it even possible for them to take up most of your eye?

"No, Facetus, no!" Hazley practically screamed. It was like she knew *exactly* what he'd do to Robert.

"Oh please don't," I said, trusting the look on Hazley's face. "The last thing I want is anyone getting hurt."

"But after what he did to you—"

"I'll just avoid him now," I told him. "Please, promise me you won't hurt him. Please, Facetus? Please?"

Reluctantly he grumbled, "Fine. I promise."

"Thank you," I said. I leaned over to hug him but I quickly jumped back. "Whoa! You're incredibly hot!" I touched his forehead. "Do you have a fever?"

"No, I'm fine," he said. I could tell he was still mad. He stood up. "Come on, Hazley." When she hesitated, he yelled, "Come on!" and they both left.

"He's so calm," Marcie said, "and then it's like you flip a switch…."

"Yeah…," I said, lost in thought about the whole situation.

I was exhausted the whole day, but I didn't even try to sleep because I knew it would feel too weird to in broad daylight.

When the evening rolled around, I found Marcie in the living room, reading something on her phone.

"Oh, this poor old lady was attacked on her front porch last night," she said.

"She was? *Oh,*" I said.

"I know, right? Ooh!" Marcie scrolled down. "Her grandkids were looking around her house this morning and claim an old necklace that belonged to her was stolen!"

"Really? How do they know?" I asked.

"They said in all their memories their grandma was wearing it. She loved it. But they can't find it anywhere in the house…."

"So, what? Someone saw she was dead and rushed into her house to steal it? That's just wrong," I said.

"Or from around her neck," Marcie said. "They said

she wore it a lot."

"Do you think the animal could've taken it?" I asked after a pause. "Like, it got caught in its fur or something?"

She shrugged. "Hey! Here's a picture of it!" We both looked at her phone screen. It was filled with an old photo of a smiling older lady with a shiny medallion hanging from her neck. "Hey, doesn't that look like—" Marcie froze.

"What?" I asked anxiously. "Marcie, what?" She was staring at my chest. I looked down. "Oh my god," I said. I undid the chain from behind my neck and held up the trinket next to the picture.

"It can't be…," I said.

"But it looks like it," Marcie said.

I held the trinket in my hand and turned it over. "Marcie, what was the name of that woman?"

"Martha Fernandaz. Why?"

I showed her the back of the trinket.

Chapter 28

"It has her name carved on the back!" Marcie exclaimed. "It's got to be the exact same one!" She paused. "But then, how did what's-his-face get it?"

"I don't know," I said. "It's all very odd.... Maybe the animal dropped it and he found it without realizing it belonged to someone else?" I hated to think of Facetus of being a thief. He would *never* do such a thing! "I mean, he *did* say he found it!"

"I wasn't accusing him of anything," Marcie said. "I was just wondering.... Well, I guess maybe we should take it to the police station so it can be returned to its rightful owner."

"Yeah." I was a little disappointed I didn't get to keep my gift for very long...but it's the right thing to do, so....

"Well, it's getting late," Marcie said, as if reading my mind, "so we can return it tomorrow."

Yay!

Oh, wait. I probably shouldn't be that excited....

What I had thought would be a quick drop-off turned into a questionare.

First of all, I was asked who I was and where I'd found it.

"My name is Maybeline Chevy," I said, "and I didn't find it. My friend did."

"Mm-hmm," the policeman said. "And where did your *friend* find it?"

"I don't know," I said, "he didn't say."

"What's his name?"

"Facetus."

"Excuse me, what?"

"Facetus. That's his name," I said. "He's not English," I explained. "I mean, not an English speaker. I mean, he *speaks* English, it's just not his first." I paused. "It's not the language spoken where he's from." There. That sounded like a good explanation.

"Mm-hmm. Where's he from?"

"Um…I'm not entirely sure."

"What is his native language?"

"I don't know. He said he doesn't know how to say it in ours."

"How long have you known him?"

"A few weeks."

"Can you give an address where we might be able to contact him?"

The questions kept coming for what seemed like *forever.* The police are very serious about their job.

The rest of the week went by in a blur. Wake up, serve coffee, sleep, repeat. I'd almost completely forgotten about the community dance this Saturday until Mom texted me about it Wednesday night. She tried to sound casual, but I knew it was just an excuse for her to ask me about Facetus.

I told her, no, he hasn't boughten me flowers. No, I haven't gone to dinner with him. And no, we don't cuddle when Marcie isn't home. It's all true, but I think she thinks I was holding back on her.

On Thursday, Robert came back to the coffee shop and bugged me about going out again. And double oh-no, Facetus came for coffee all in the middle of it.

"I'm just saying that sometimes things aren't perfect," Robert was saying, "and last Friday was one of those things and—"

"Hey, Maybes," Facetus said as he came in. "The ushe, please." His face came to life. "Did I use it right? I just learned it!"

"Good for you!" I smiled. "Yep, you're a superstar! Coming right up!"

Robert eyed Facetus suspiciously. He cleared his throat impatiently. "As I was saying, last Friday had some kinks, but this time it'll be *perfect.*" Facetus lost his smile and now it was his turn to glare at the other boy.

Oh no, I thought.

"We can go out to dinner again—any place you want. And then we can go back to—"

"No!" I couldn't help the abruptness of my voice. *Calm down. Don't want to start a fight between Robert and Facetus.* "I mean, *no,* Robert. I *will not* go out with you again, no matter where or when, I will *not.*"

"But—"

"She said no, *Robert!*" Facetus's voice was beginning to drop.

Somebody pinch me so I can wake up.

Chapter 29

"Oh, I'm sorry, are you *a part* of this conversation?" Robert asked coldly.

"I am now!" Facetus said.

I laughed nervously. "O.K. now. Let's not overreact—"

"There is no overreaction about what he did to you, Maybeline!" Facetus said.

"About what I—" Robert said. He turned to me. "You're going around telling people? You're making me sound like a bad person?"

"You are a bad person!" Facetus said.

"She was ready, she just didn't know it!" Robert yelled at him.

"You guys—" I said.

"She told you no!" Facetus said. "And it's *her* decision whether or not she's ready!"

"—people are staring—"

"What are you? Her boyfriend?" Robert said. "Protective older brother?"

"—you're making a scene!" I squeaked, letting my arms slide across the countertop and dropping my head so I didn't have to watch.

"None of the above," Facetus said. I couldn't help peeking. He stepped closer to Robert so he was in his face. "I'm your worst nightmare. So lay off her. And if you don't, you're going to have to answer to *me*. And you don't want that."

"Don't tell me what I want," Robert said.

"I know what you want," Facetus said. "And you *don't* want that."

"What are you, a ninja?" Robert mockingly asked.

"I'm worse," Facetus answered. *"Much worse."*

"And what, I'm supposed to *be afraid* of you?" Facetus's menacing tone hadn't phased Robert.

"You touch her and you're dead, playboy," Facetus said. *"Dead."*

"What if she *wants* me to touch her?"

"That would be all right," Facetus replied. "But that's not the case, is it?"

"All right," I said in an overly bright tone. "Facetus, why don't you take your cappuccino, your *ushe*," I made use of his new word, "and skedaddle outta here, and Robert can make his way home too, O.K.?"

Facetus turned to me. "I'm going to *what* out of here?"

"Skedaddle," I said. He stared at me. I started to

slowly run in place.

"Why didn't you just say 'run'?" he said.

"I was trying to be fun," I said. "You know, kind of like how you said 'ushe.'"

"Yeah well, I'm done being fun." He took his cappuccino and set his money on the counter. "I'll go when he goes." He looked at Robert.

"I'm not going anywhere," Robert said.

"Yes, you are." Facetus stared into Robert. Robert's eyes widened and he quickly bolted for the door. When he was gone, Facetus said to me, "If he bothers you again, let me know." He turned to go.

"But, Facetus," I said, "you promised."

He stopped. "I promised to you avoiding him and not seeing him again," he said over his shoulder. "Things are different now." And then he was gone.

And I was left with a whole shop full of customers staring at me.

I smiled sheepishly as I looked around, trying to make the situation look better than it was, then practically ran and hid in the back room for a few minutes and waited for conversation in the shop to spark up again.

Chapter 30

Bring. Bring. Bring.
I rolled over and picked up my phone.
"Hello?" I mumbled.
Bring.
Oh right. I have to press a button to answer. It's *way* too early in the morning for a phone call.
"Hello?" I said after lots of aimless tapping.
"Is this Maybeline Chevy?" a gruff voice asked.
"Yeah...."
"Well, we're going to have to have you bring your friend in to the station later to answer questions because we can't find the name you gave us in the town records."
"Oh, O.K.," I said. Facetus must live in the next town or something. "Yeah, I can do that. I'll bring him by after work?"
"Sure, that works. What time do you get off?"
"Four."
"Great."
I got up and went to tell Marcie, who was already in the kitchen.
"Hmm," was Marcie's answer.

"What?" I asked.

"I don't know," she said. "I don't trust whatever-his-name-is."

"What do you mean?" I couldn't believe she was saying that.

"He just 'happened to find it' when the little old lady *always* had it with her?"

"What, are you accusing him of being the attacker behind all of this? Because he would neve—"

"No, it's an animal," Marcie said. "But maybe he knows more than he's letting on?" Her tone sounded very suggestive and I didn't like it. "For instance, how did he know they're happening at night? Even *now* the police aren't sure. Don't you think it's a little…"—she hesitated—"suspicious?"

"What? *No!*" I said. "Facetus would *never*—"

"I know," Marcie said. She remained silent, but I knew she had more to add. I couldn't even *think* of Facetus being involved in such a thing! I mean, he would *never* do something like that.

Would he?

"So, how are you going to contact what's-his-face?" Marcie asked as I was getting ready to leave. "You don't have his number or his address or anything, do you?"

"No," I said, "but yesterday he told me to tell him if Robert bothers me again, so I would assume he'd be hanging around the coffee shop or something…." I *hoped* he'd be hanging around the coffee shop or something, because then what'd I tell the police after I'd promised to bring him?

"'Hanging around the coffee shop or something'?" Marcie looked at me incredulously.

"You didn't see him yesterday," I said. "I wouldn't be surprised if he's on patrol." I told her about his and Robert's not-so-little dispute.

"Jeez," Marcie said. "You didn't tell me that."

"I didn't want to talk about it," I told her. And Marcie hadn't noticed anything wrong because I hadn't had my mind on it. I was busy worrying about what I was going to tell my mom about the dance tomorrow. *Tomorrow.* Ahh! Just got to get it over with. Mom worries about me not socializing enough, so I would have to go. And she would know too because it's a *community* dance and she's one of the organization's volunteers this year.

* * *

When I made it to the first floor, I was so unluckily greeted by the elderly.

"Hey, young girl," Mr. Rockwell yelled to me. "Was there some boy with you the other weekend?"

"Stop yelling at that coatrack!" Ms. Fellers said.

"She ain't no coatrack!" he yelled at her. "Tell her you ain't no coatrack!" he said to me.

"I'm not a coatrack, Ms. Fellers," I said calmly.

"Yeah well, I don't trust talking woodwork!" she said.

"But there was some boy with you," Mr. Rockwell said. "I'm not 'seeing things.'" He made an eyeroll to Ms. Fellers. "For the last two weeks she ain't been believing me!" he said to me.

"I have had some friends over," I said. "Now, I *really* need to get going...." I quickly made a run for the door. I felt bad about leaving when they were still trying to talk to me, but at least I told them I was going, right?

Chapter 31

I hurriedly turned my body to close the door and started running ahead before I'd fully turned around and, with my luck, misjudged the distance to the steps and tripped.

I waited for that painful sting as I fell. But to my surprise, it never came.

"You really need to start watching where you're going, Bels."

I gripped the arms that had caught me as I righted my feet on the ground, breathing hard. What I'd just so miraculously missed….

And what I'd just so miraculously found.

"Facetus," I said as we released our lock on each other, "what are you doing here?"

"Well…." He hesitated. "I just came by…to see how you're doing…you went blippity-bloppity-bloo and I stopped you from going blunk, so…yeah."

"Well, thank you for saving me from going…*blunk*." I laughed. "Come on, I still want to talk to you," I said as I walked around the building. "So, you know that necklace you gave me?"

"Oh, yes, with the horse," he said. "What about it?"

"Well," I said, getting in my car. I motioned to him to go on the other side. I closed my door once he had opened the passenger side. "It turned out it belonged to a little old lady who was attacked."

"Oh yes," he said, "the one knitting on her porch."

"Knitting?" I turned to him. "Put your seat belt on," I told him. He gave me a look of annoyance but put it on anyway. "What do you mean knitting?" I asked again.

"I mean she was knitting on her porch before she was attacked," he said as I pulled out.

"But I didn't see anything about that," I said, putting on my turn signal. "Where did you read that?"

"Um, anyway…," he said as I pulled out onto the road. "What about the necklace?"

"It belonged to someone else, so I gave it to the police to give to her grandkids, who were looking for it," I said.

"Oh."

"And I need you to come with me to the police station after work to answer questions since I don't know where exactly you found it."

He was silent. "O.K.," he said eventually.

"Well, I mean, it's not that I don't appreciate your gift," I said, "it's just I saw they were in search of it, and so I thought it'd be the right thing to do to give it to them. You know, since it belonged to their grandma and all."

"Right," he said. I quickly glanced at him. He was staring at his hands in his lap. I hoped I hadn't hurt his feelings.

"You know, Buddy really missed you," I said, trying to lighten the mood.

"Who?" Facetus said.

"Buddy," I said. "My dog. After you and Hazley left, he was sniffing all around. I think he was upset to have missed you. You see, he was napping on my bed when you came."

"Oh," he said. "He didn't wake up?"

"No, he's a very sound sleeper for a dog," I said. "Very odd, isn't it? Once he's out, he's out."

"Oh." Facetus forced a laugh.

Silence.

Oh, why'd I have to hurt the feelings of such a wonderful person?

"Maybeline?" Facetus's gentle voice knocked me out of my thoughts.

"Yeah?" I asked, full of guilt.

"Um…." He paused. "The reason I came over this

morning...."

"Was to check on me?" I finished. "See how I was doing?"

"Um...no, not exactly," he said.

I was in such suspense at his pauses. It was like he was telling me an exciting story. Except this was a real-life conversation.

"You see...I, um...," he said. "So, I was thinking and, um...I was *feeling* like, uh...."

"What?" I was almost to work and I couldn't stand the anticipation!

"Like, um...like I, uh...needed to, um...tell you...something...."

"What?"

"I, uh...I'm...I'm...." He ran his fingers through his hair. Wait, I'm not supposed to know that! *Eyes on the road, Chevy!* "So I...I...."

"Work's right ahead, so you better tell me, Facetus," I said quickly as the coffee place came into view.

"I...I...I'm sorry!" he spat out as if it was a confession. "I'm sorry I got all upset over Robert and threatened and yelled when you didn't want me to and upset you and I upset Hazley and I'm just sorry, O.K.!"

He had to take a moment to catch his breath.

I stopped the car.

"It's O.K., Facetus," I said, looking at him, "you didn't upset me, it's just that you were making a scene and I wanted you to stop."

He slowly turned to me like he was afraid. "But you asked me to stop and I didn't," he said quietly.

"It's O.K.," I said softly, "you were just looking out for me. I appreciate that." I put my hand on his shoulder. "Are you always that warm?" I asked, removing my hand and thinking. Were his kisses warm? I couldn't quite recall as they were fast moments. Was he that warm when I was on his motorcycle? Well, yes, but I hadn't thought much about it before because of the heat from the engine and the summer sun. "Is that even healthy?" I asked.

"Um…," he said, looking in the distance.

"Are you ill?" I touched his forehead.

"No, I-I'm O.K.," he said.

"Are you sure? Do you need to see a doctor? Fevers are bad, you know. They can mess with your brain—"

"Yes, yes, I know," he said, finally looking at me. "I'm fine. Thank you, Maybeline."

"O.K.," I said. "Well, if you need me to take you, I can."

"O.K.," he said. "Thank you."

Chapter 32

"All right, I'm going to go to work now," I said, getting out of the car. Facetus followed me five seconds later.

"Sorry, you're not stranded, are you?" I said. I couldn't believe I hadn't thought about what he was going to do when I got to work. Typical me. Just thinking about now and not later.

"No…," he said slowly. "I'm still in the city…just like you…."

"Sorry, I meant, you're O.K. being here? You don't need to be anywhere else?"

"No," he shrugged. "I have nothing going on. I can go inside with you if you'd like?"

"Sure," I said, going up to the door. "Do you want coffee?"

"Mm…I had some yesterday so I probably shouldn't today. Thank you," he said.

"O.K."

We went inside.

"Chevy, there you are!" Mr. Saperstien said. "Come. We've got some early bird customers to serve!"

I rushed back behind the counter and got to work.

After I got my name tag and apron on, I quickly started on the orders. I noticed Facetus had picked up a newspaper and was leafing through it. "Hmm," I heard him say.

"Looking for something specific?" I asked him.

"Nah," he said, putting it down. "I was just looking at the attacks."

"They're awful, right?" I said.

"Yes," he agreed. "I wish they'd stop."

"Me too," I said. "I wish they knew what kind of animal it was."

"Probably a bear or something," Facetus said.

"No," I said, "it's not a bear. They examined the DNA and it's something we haven't discovered yet."

"What do you mean? What DNA?" He looked worried.

"Oh, the animal broke some sort of ornament in one of the victims' houses and there was a bit of blood left on some of the pieces, and they had scientists examine it for information, which didn't prove to be much help other than scaring us more, so…." I didn't know where I was going with this.

"Maybeline?"

I looked at Facetus. He looked scared.

"What? What's wrong? What is it?"

"I—What are we going to do at the police station?"

"Answer questions about the necklace you found," I said. "Are you all right?"

"Y-yes, I just…," he said, "need to step outside for some fresh air. I think you're right, I do have a fever." He quickly dashed out the door.

My lunch break came and Facetus still hadn't come back. Concerned, I went outside to see if I could find him.

"Facetus?" I called. I searched all around but I couldn't find him. I ate lunch and finished up my shift, still thinking about him.

Now what am I going to tell the police? I thought as I drove to the station. As I was walking to the door, I was surprised to hear his voice. What are the odds?

"Oh, Maybeline! Oh, I am so sorry! Oh, I shouldn't have left you at the coffee house; that was very wrong of me to do! Oh, I am so sorry!"

"Facetus, it's O.K.," I said.

"No, it's not O.K.! Don't forgive me! I'm awful! I'm absolutely awful! I'm so bad! I'm such a bad friend! I don't deserve you!"

"No, Facetus," I said, "you're a wonderful friend."

"No, I'm not!" he said. "I'm a terrible friend!" He looked like he might cry at any moment.

"You're the best friend I've ever had!" Well, except for Marcie. I hugged him. "You're kind, you're caring, you're sweet...I love you." Whoa, where did that come from?

"You wouldn't say that if you knew," he said.

"If I knew what?" I looked up at his face.

"Are you two here for something?"

I quickly stepped back from Facetus and looked at the officer who'd just exited the building. "Oh, uh, yeah, yeah, we are," I said. "We're here for, um, to do, uh—"

"To talk about a necklace," Facetus said.

"Right, right," I said. The officer looked at me suspiciously before leading us into the building and down some halls to where we were to be questioned —well, Facetus. I'd already had my interrogation.

"What is your name?" the lieutenant asked.

"Facetus," Facetus answered.

"Pardon?"

"Facetus," he answered. "That's my name."

"Last?"

"What?"

"What is your last name?"

Facetus stared blankly at him.

"Your last name," I said. "The name that comes after yours and everybody in your family."

He still didn't say anything.

"He doesn't speak English," I explained to the lieutenant.

"I speak English, Maybeline," Facetus said as if I was a little kid failing to understand a lesson time after time.

"Well, I know, but it's not your first," I said.

"What is your first language?" the lieutenant asked Facetus.

"I don't know," he answered.

"You don't know?"

"I mean, I don't know what it's called in your language."

"O.K. What is your contact info, in case we need to contact you?"

"Uh…." Facetus appeared to be at a loss.

"Like, what's your phone number and your address?" I said. Good thing I'd come with him.

"I don't have a phone," Facetus said, "and I don't have a designated address. I'm always moving."

"Is that so?" the lieutenant said.

"Yes," Facetus said. "I like to see different places."

"So, you're not going to be here for much longer?" I knew it was off subject, but I couldn't help asking.

"Maybe a couple more weeks," he told me.

Well, my emotional rollercoaster just dropped about thirty feet.

"So, you don't have any permanent location?" the lieutenant continued.

"No," Facetus said.

"Well, can you give us the name of any close family member we can contact then?"

"No," Facetus said.

"Any family member?"

Facetus shook his head.

"Friend?"

Facetus looked at me.

"Maybeline," he said.

Chapter 33

I was his contact person? Not a family member?

"All right," the lieutenant said. "Let's get down to what we called you here for. Where was the exact location you found the necklace?"

"I don't know," Facetus said. "It was in someone's yard."

"You were trespassing on others' property?"

"No, I was walking and saw it where the grass was sidewalk."

"'Where the grass was sidewalk'?"

"Yes," he said. "It was where the grass stopped…at the sidewalk."

"O.K. Whose house was it at?"

"I don't remember."

"Did it ever occur to you that you could've been stealing?"

"I just thought it was some sort of cheap toy…," he said. "Something disposable that just missed the trash."

"And you gave that cheap, disposable thing to this young lady as a gift?"

"I asked a friend if they wanted anything with it

before I threw it away, and they said they thought Maybie would like it."

"That maybe *who* would like it?"

"Maybie," he said. "Maybeline." He gestured to me.

"Mm-hmm," the lieutenant said. "And did you notice a name on the back of the little horse charm?"

"Uh, no, I didn't," Facetus said.

"Why don't you be more careful next time you find something that doesn't belong to you?"

Facetus nodded.

When all the questioning was finally over, it was dark out and the streetlights were on.

"Do you want me to drive you home?" I asked Facetus.

"Nah, it's O.K.," he said.

"You sure?" I asked, opening my car door.

"Yeah, I could use the fresh air." He smiled under the fluorescence.

"O.K. Wait," I said as he turned to go. I stepped out away from my car and kissed him on the lips. "Bye," I said. I got in my car and started the engine. I could see him reluctantly smile like he still felt guilty and "undeserving of me" but couldn't help being happy I still cared about him and wanted to be his friend.

There was hardly any traffic on the drive home. I had just pulled on to a residential road lined with parked cars when I had to stomp on the brakes to avoid hitting a figure who'd just emerged from the darkness.

The figure froze in the headlights and I honked the horn to try to get them to move. But the figure stayed in his position, one foot on the left of the dividing line, the other on the right. It was dark, and the headlights didn't quite illuminate his features, so I couldn't identify who it was.

"Excuse me," I said, opening my door. "Could you please move?" As I walked, I could see both my shadows ahead of me. "Excuse me," I said again as I neared the person. "You see, I'm driving someplace and, well, you're kind of in my way. So if you could just mo—"

Suddenly, the figure reached out and grabbed me!

"See, Maybeline? We did meet again. And this time, it's going to be *perfect.*"

"No! Let go of me, Robert!" I screamed, struggling in his grip. I kicked him in the shin, causing him to release his grip in pain. But as I turned around, he quickly caught my wrist like a reflex.

"Oh, don't go yet, baby," he said in an odd tone. It almost sounded tired.

"No, let go of me!"

"She told you to let go of her, dimwit."

Facetus!

"You can't tell me what to do!" Robert said. "Maybeline is *mine,* and you can't stop me!"

"Want to bet?"

"You don't want to fight me," Robert said.

"Let her go!" Facetus demanded.

I still struggled against Robert. He had a death lock on my arm and I can't tell you how much it hurt!

"Robert, let go!" I cried. "You're hurting me!"

Facetus grabbed Robert's arm and stared him straight in the eyes. "You let go of her *right now,* you little son of—"

Robert shrieked and the piercing pain on my wrist ceased.

I tried to examine my wrist for marks, but the headlights weren't bright enough for me to do so.

"Maybeline! Are you all right?" I felt Facetus's warm hands on my shoulders.

"I…I…." I couldn't make out any words. I buried my face in his chest and sobbed. I felt his arms slowly wrap around me as if he was hesitant. But I'm glad he did because I felt oddly secure and safe in his arms, like he was invincible and no danger would befall me as long as I was with him. "How did you get here so fast?" I asked. "How did you know I needed help?"

"I heard you scream and hurried here as quick as I could," he said.

"But you were so far away…," I said.

"My hearing's in good condition and I'm a fast runner," he replied.

"Oh, so you think you can have her all to yourself now, huh?" Robert interrupted. "Mr. Hero saves the day again. What do you see in him, Maybeline? Tell me."

"Go home, Robert!" I cried.

"I won't go home until you're *mine.*"

Facetus turned his body so that I was hidden from Robert.

"Come on!" Robert said, grabbing Facetus's shoulder and jerking him around so that he faced him square. "Fight for her *like a man."*

"Come on, Facetus," I said, "let's go."

But Facetus didn't answer me. I was behind him, so I couldn't see his face, but I could see him stiffen.

"Come on, Facetus!" I said again.

Robert took one step forward.

Facetus burst into a run and shoved the other boy backward. Robert stood up and threw a punch at him —which Facetus timelessly caught before it hit his face. He twisted the other boy's arm in an impossible curve before throwing him down to the concrete.

"You guys, stop!" I screamed. "Facetus, leave it alone! Let's just go!"

But Facetus didn't listen.

He picked the other boy up by the shirt collar and said in the most frightening tone I'd ever heard in my life, "I will rip your throat out before you even have the reflex to scream, you stupid, selfish—"

"Facetus, stop!" I cried. "This isn't like you!"

And it wasn't.

For when he turned to me, I was looking straight into the eyes of a monster.

Chapter 34

I took a step back and gasped.

The eyes that looked into mine were hollow—it could've just been the way the light hit his face, but still…. His face in general seemed off…not round and smooth like a human face, but harder and flatter looking, like he was wearing a mask.

Shakily, I tried to take in the rest of his body in the darkness. He appeared to be skinnier and bonier than usual and he had a bit of a slouch. Maybe it's just the darkness that makes him look that way? No…no one has fingers that long and nails that sharp….

"You're the thing that's been killing everyone!" I screamed as I came to the realization.

Facetus dropped Robert without taking his eyes off me. He started to me. "Maybeline, I—"

"No!" I screamed. He paused in his step. "No, just stay away from me! Just stay away!"

"Maybeline!" He came after me again. He was starting to look normal again.

"No!" I screamed and ran to my car.

Crap, passenger side.

Maybe he'd follow me if I went around the back.

Then I'd get to the driver side before he.

And he did follow me, just as I'd hoped.

"Maybeline, I just want to talk to you!" he said.

"No, stay away!" I slammed the driver door shut and locked it along with the other doors. I went into reverse and quickly backed out of the street and chose a different route home, leaving that horrible nightmare behind me.

When I got home, Marcie was already asleep. It's just like her to carefully plan bedtime. I went to bed and tried to clear my head, but that image of Facetus in an unexplainable form kept taking up my vision—whether my eyes were opened or closed.

I barely got any sleep that night, having nightmare after nightmare about what had happened. If only it *was* just a big nightmare, not the undeniable truth.

I groggily came out into the kitchen, giving up on any sort of rest.

"Good morning," Marcie said. "How did you sleep? How was the police station? Did you find what's-his-face?"

"Yeah and I wish I hadn't." I tiredly sat at the counter.

"How come?" Marcie asked. Her face became very serious. "What did he do to you? Tell me, what did he do?"

"Nothing to me, but—"

I was interrupted by a pounding at the door. Marcie answered it. "Hello, Ms. Chevy," she said. "How are you this morning?"

"Today's the community dance," my mom said. "So I need to get my daughter and—oh my guacamole, what happened to you?" my mom said, looking at me. "You look like you got hit by ten garbage trucks and attacked by a pack of mice. Come on, baby. Why aren't you ready? The dance starts at ten thirty and I have to be there at ten. Come on, let's get moving!"

And so, for the next half hour my mom and my roommate helped me get ready as quickly as possible.

"O.K., it's nine forty-three," my mom said, checking the time. "We need to move. Are you coming to the dance, Marcie?"

"No, Ms. Chevy, I'm staying home," Marcie said.

"O.K. Let's get moving, kiddo."

I followed my mom out the door.

When we arrived, Mom went to help the other

volunteers set up, so I was left all alone for a little while. While I waited I observed the ancient building. It had been years since I'd last been here, when Mom used to drive me here back when I lived at home. I'd never realized how beautiful the ballroom was—probably because just like all the other young people who'd populated the dance floor, I was just trying to figure out *how* exactly to dance with a partner since nobody had ever shown me.

The fine woodwork of the entire room had been varnished and had a glistening glow in the light. The tall round ceiling was decorated with large stained-glass windows with red, blue, green, and yellow patterns of triangles and circles.

I was in such awe over the beauty that I barely noticed when people started arriving. Before I knew it, the whole dance floor was filled with people. Some were dancing and others were helping themselves to the refreshments table my mom and the other volunteers had set up.

"Hey, baby girl."

I turned at the sound of my mom's voice.

"I was in charge of making the homemade chip dip. You'll have to let me know how it is."

"O.K., will do, Mom," I said.

"Great!" She gave me two thumbs up before going back into the crowd.

I made my way through the sea of people to the table. Most of the people who'd gotten refreshments had already made their way back to the dance floor and the rest were just finishing up, so I was by myself grabbing chips from a bag and dipping them in my mom's dip.

But I wasn't solitary for very long.

"Hey, Maybeline," I heard a soft voice next to me say.

I paused with my first chip in the container of dip.

"I just want to talk to you. Can we, please?"

I finally pulled the chip up out of the dip and took a bite, pretending I hadn't heard him. But it was too late to play that game because my elongated pause had already let him know I was listening.

"I don't expect anything from you. I just want to explain to you about what happened last night."

I silently continued eating chips. Mom did a good job on the dip; I'd have to tell her later.

"Maybeline, can you speak to me?"

I grabbed another chip.

"I just want to know what's going on in your head. What are you thinking? What do you think about last night? What do you think about everything in general? Please, I want to know…so I can help you…a-and explain any questions you may have. Please, just talk to me."

I slowly turned my head with caution. Those amber eyes looked so pleading, so yearning for my attention.

"Please, Maybeline." Facetus's golden eyes stared desperately into mine.

"Fine," I said. "Fine, you want to tell me why you're killing everyone? Why you're hurting all those innocent people? Why you're—"

"Shh, shh, shh." Facetus held up his hands for me to calm down. "No no no no no, Maybeline." He quickly glanced around the room. I don't think anyone would have heard me anyway over the music.

"You asked me what I was thinking." I felt like I would cry at any moment.

"I know, and I will answer your questions," he said. He started to the floor and then stopped to look at me. "Come, dance with me."

"I'm not dancing with you," I said firmly.

He smiled for the first time. "It *is* a dance, and I

don't see you dancing with anybody else, so…."

I crossed my arms and glared at him. He struggled not to laugh. "I'll tell you everything," he said. "Promise." I rolled my eyes. "Come," he said, holding out his hand. "I don't bite…." He grinned wickedly at me.

I sighed. "Fine," I grumbled, taking his hand. I felt like I was walking into a trap but at the same time dodging a bullet.

Chapter 35

The person whose arms I once felt the most secure and safe in I now felt the most anxious and terrified in.

"So?" I said, trying to keep my tone straight. "Are you going to tell me?"

"I guess that depends on what you want me to tell you," Facetus answered.

"I thought you were going to tell me everything," I said.

"I wouldn't know where to start with everything."

I paused, thinking. "Why are you killing everyone?" I could barely get the words out. "What did they ever do to you?"

"I'm not killing…everybody," he said.

"Then who? And why, Facetus, why? You seem like such a nice person…." I felt a single tear run down my cheek.

"Oh, don't cry, child." He wiped it off my face with his thumb. "I have nothing against those people."

"Then—then why—" I choked out.

"I'm not killing them." We'd stopped dancing. He held my face in his hands. "I'm not." Then he brushed my mom's perfect curls off my shoulders. "I would…."

I heard some guffawing in the distance. I looked over and saw Robert and his clan in the doorway. When they turned in my direction, I quickly looked away and jumped up to kiss Facetus.

"...do care about—" His words were cut off when my lips hit his.

"Sorry, baby, you were saying?" I tried my best smile as I ran my fingers through his hair. He stared at me in disbelief. I slowly let my smile fade and let my hands fall from his hair to his shoulders, down his chest, then off him completely. He continued to stare at me, eyes wide and jaw dropped. I carefully stole a glance in Robert's direction. He wasn't paying any attention to me; just arguing with his troop. When I turned back to Facetus, he still looked shocked...like crazy-woman-in-the-coffee-shop shocked. But he didn't offer me any help this time. He just continued to stare at me.

"Facetus?" I said. *"Hello?"*

"I-I, um, yeah? Hello?" he barely made out.

"You all right?" I had to admit I was a little amused by his reaction.

"Y-y-yes," he said. "Y-yes, I'm...all right...." He put his hands in his pockets and looked at the ceiling. I wondered if he admired the artwork too.

"You were saying...?" I said.

He looked at me. "I-I was saying...w-what was I... saying?"

"You were going to tell me everything."

"Right, right," he said. "What have I already told you?"

"Nothing," I said. "Except you didn't kill anybody."

"Right, right." He looked at the ground.

"Are you all right?" I was really concerned this time.

"Yes, *yes,* I'm all right." He looked up at me. He didn't sound all right. I felt like I had some explaining to do myself.

"You know, I, um," I said, "I did that because... Robert was...looking in my direction, and...." I thought the rest was self explanatory.

"All his friends think he's nuts, so...." He laughed a little.

"How do you know?" I asked.

"I can hear them," he said.

"From across the room?" I glanced at Robert's group.

"Yes," Facetus said. "In fact, I can hear every conversation in this room."

"Every conversation?" He nodded. "Even over the music?"

"Yes, even over the music," he said.

"Well, why do they think he's nuts? What are they saying?"

"They think he's got a screw loose because he's been babbling on about some *monster* that attacked him last night." Facetus genuinely laughed this time.

"Well, some monster *did* attack him last night," I said.

"Come here," he said, wrapping his arms around my waist. "This is one of my favorite songs." He led me through a series of intricate steps.

"Whoa, where did you learn to dance?" I laughed.

"Colonial America," he replied. "But I've picked up on a few modern steps over the years, so things might get a bit *wild.*" He spun me in a double twirl before pulling me back to him. I laughed into his chest. I'd forgotten for a few minutes what a monster he is. He laughed too. "Oh, thank you for dancing with me, Maybie," he said, stroking my hair. "I haven't had this much fun in a long time."

"We're done?" I looked up at him. Ah, I actually wanted to dance with him some more.

He smiled at me. "I actually didn't think you'd put up with me this long."

"You didn't?"

"No, I didn't," he said. "It's more than worth it now. I was afraid I'd showered for nothing."

"Do you not normally shower?" I asked slowly. We were rocking back and forth now.

"I don't really like it," he said. "That's why I haven't in so many years."

I stopped dancing. "You haven't showered since I've met you?"

"No, I did this morning," he said. "What?"

"That's disgusting," I said. "That's something an animal would do."

"Speaking of which," he said, leading me into another dance routine. He dipped me backward. "Let's talk about that."

Chapter 36

Facetus pulled me up and grasped my right hand with his. He began walking in circles around me, pulling me so that I was walking around him too.

"First of all," he said, "it may be obvious to you that I'm not like you or any other humans."

"Right," I said, remembering the night before.

"That's because I'm not…human." He dropped my one hand and picked the other up with his left hand and led me in the other direction.

I felt a chill go through my body.

"Not…human?"

"No, I only pretend to be," he said.

"Then wha—what are you?" We changed hands again.

"I suppose I'd be what you'd call…a vampire," he said. "But not what you'd think; we're just what your stories are loosely based on. We don't really dine on flesh while drinking human blood."

"You eat flesh!" I dropped his hand and stepped back.

"Oh, do you not tell those anymore?"

"No, you just drink blood."

"What do we eat?"

"Nothing. Just blood."

"That's odd. Anyway, it's like any other of your tales. They're just loosely based on something you didn't understand." He bowed to me. He looked up, then pulled me down by my shoulder to his level.

"So, witches aren't what we think?" I asked as we stood upright again. "What about werewolves? What are they?"

He grabbed my right hand and we went into our routine again. "Let's talk about one thing at a time," he said. "When the humans evolved and built their civilizations, they caused many problems for all the other creatures—especially the vampires."

"Why the vampires?" I asked as we changed direction.

"Do you know how the plants eat the sun, the rabbits eat the plants, and the foxes eat the rabbits?" I nodded. "The plants eat the sun, the deer eat the plants, the humans eat the deer, guess what eats the humans."

I paused in the middle of the hand change.

"You eat *humans?*" I asked in shock as he began guiding me again.

"Not much anymore," he said. "But it takes much more rabbits or deer or foxes than it does humans for us to not be hungry. When the humans evolved"—we switched hands again—"the vampires had to. They couldn't just walk into the human civilization; there were too many to fight and besides, they had their crazy weapons that made it close to impossible, so they learned mimicry." He bowed to me again. I was in synch with him this time.

When I reached to grasp his hand again, he said, "Let's try it without touching hands this time."

"Without touching?"

"Yes," he said. "I was just making the first two rounds easy for you."

"Well, how do we do that?" I asked.

"Like this," he said, holding up my right arm with his left hand and placing his right hand just an inch in front of mine. "We walk around each other just like before, except our hands stay like this; close but not touching." He let go of my right arm.

"O.K." I struggled to keep a one-inch distance. My hand bumped his every second. "Who danced like this?" I asked. "Like, what time?"

"Nineteenth century," he replied, lowering his one

hand and raising the other.

"So, you were around back then?" I asked.

"Yes," he said. "Vampires have a longer life span than humans."

"How old are you?" I asked as we switched sides.

"Mm...I don't want to talk about that," he said. "Then you'd think I'm old. Besides, I stopped keeping track of my age years ago. I suppose compared to a vampire's life span, I'd be about middle aged."

"You? Middle aged?" I laughed. "You look like you're seventeen." We switched hands again.

"Seventeen? Really?" he laughed.

"Well, that's a bit of an exaggeration, but I think you could pass for it," I said.

"That's still quite the compliment," he said, bowing to me. "I don't think anyone's said something that nice to me in a long time." We held up our hands and started circling again.

"What? Isn't that a part of your mimicry? Can't you make yourself look younger?"

"No," he replied. "Just change a few features and shapes of our limbs."

"So, this is what you'd look like if you were human?" I looked him up and down.

"Not exactly"—we switched hands—"but in general, yes. I have to change myself a bit to look human, so it's not perfect. But if I was, yes, I'd look very similar. That's what I went to school for: to look and act like a human. Now we do both." He lined up his right hand with my left and his left with my right as we circled again, still not touching.

"You had to learn?" I asked. "You couldn't just do that?"

"I could, but to make sure it's perfect, we have other people teach us. It's not good if a human sees through your disguise."

"What kind of people taught you that?" Instead of going the other way again, he took me in his arms and led me through a waltz.

"Older vampires who were assigned the teaching role," he replied.

"Oh, I thought *people* taught you how to do it." I laughed at my mistake.

"We're not important enough to be called people?" he asked.

"I suppose that's true." I hadn't really thought about it.

"Why not? Why aren't we important enough?" He

seemed truly troubled by this question.

"No, I mean, that's true, you should be important enough. You *are* important enough," I added. "Can you become any animal you want?" I asked.

"Sure, with a little practice," he said. "But humans are usually the only creatures who actually believe our act because of their loss of instincts."

"So that's why Buddy didn't like you!" I said.

"Yes, he could sense I was different from the start," he said. "And quite possibly a predator to you and the girl that you live with."

"Wow, he was just trying to protect me!" I said.

"Yes, dogs can be loyal companions," he said. "I do believe he'd protect you from any danger." Then he let me drop back farther than I'd ever been dipped before as the last note in the song sounded. I could barely hear the next song playing, though, as I was surrounded with the sound of applause.

Chapter 37

Facetus placed his free hand on my back between my shoulder blades and pulled me up. I looked around. I hadn't realized we'd had an audience. I wondered if they could hear our conversation. But why would Facetus tell me all that stuff in front of all those people?

Facetus stepped back away from the attention as many people I hadn't seen since high school and a few strangers gathered around me to quiz me on how I'd done all that. I actually hadn't realized our dance had been remarkable—I just followed whatever Facetus showed me…he's a great teacher! I didn't even realize I was being taught…!

There were so many questions being thrown at me that I either couldn't make them out or I didn't have enough time to answer them, so I excused myself and went into the bathroom to give myself a moment to breathe.

I looked at my reflection in the mirror and closed my eyes as I exhaled slowly.

Yes, that's nice. Peace, quiet, relaxation—

"Are you all right?"

My eyes flew open and I jumped and gasped in surprise. I saw Facetus's face behind me in the mirror and I anxiously turned around. But as I was turning, my high heel rubbed and twisted against the damp floor and I fell backward.

"Ah!" I exclaimed as the back of my head hit the sink. I was in so much surprise that the pain wasn't as sharp as it should've been. I knew I'd really feel it later though.

"You may just be the clumsiest person I have ever met," Facetus said. "And you know 'ever met' is a lot." He picked me up off the floor. "Are you O.K.?" he asked me.

"Yeah...," I said, touching my head.

"Are you sure?"

"Yeah," I sighed. "You know, I don't think you're supposed to be in here," I told him. I hoped no one had seen him walk into the girls' bathroom.

He shrugged. "I'll sense if someone's coming."

"Are you O.K.? You left rather quickly," he said.

"Yeah, I'm fine. I just needed to breathe, that's all." And I let myself take a breather then as I gathered my thoughts together.

What had I learned? Facetus was a vampire but

pretended to be a person so he could eat…people. He's been around for hundreds of years, and he can shape-shift and he eats…people….

I felt myself shaking.

"Maybeline?" I heard Facetus say. "Maybeline! What's wrong?"

"I can't…w-what if…I…you…!" It was hard to get the words out. I realized then that I was hyperventilating.

"What? What is it, Maybeline?"

"What if a vampire…and I…what if they…how… don't die…how do I…what—"

"Hey hey, Maybeline. Calm down," Facetus said. "What is it?"

"And I don't know…," I sobbed. "How do I— Facetus, tell me! Tell me! How do I know? How do I—" I paused, looking up at his face. I screamed. "You're going to—you're going to—I'm going to—why! Oh my god. Oh my god, you're going to kill me. Oh, oh my, oh —"

"Maybeline, no! I'm not going to kill you, no. I would never—hey. Hey, you listen to me. Hey. I am never, ever, *ever* going to kill you. *Ever.* O.K.? O.K.?" He made me look at him. "O.K.?"

I heard my breathing slow as I lost energy to be upset. He let go of my face and I let my head drop.

"I love you, Maybeline. I would *never* do anything to hurt you, O.K.?"

"But how do I—how do I know if someone's a vampire and what do I do if...if...!"

"Maybeline, you are not going to get attacked by a vampire," he said. "First of all, there are only about five vampires left in the entire world. And even if one of them tried to attack you, I would be there to make sure that didn't happen. And I would be there to protect you, Maybeline. O.K.? I would be there *for you.*"

"Do you promise?"

"I promise," he said.

"But how do I know you—you won't...that you're not using me, that you're not pretending, how do I—"

"That's true. That's what happens a lot of the time," he said. "A vampire *will* pretend to be friends with a human to gain their trust, and then get them alone in some room and...." He trailed off as he realized he was describing the scene happening right now. "But even if I was pretending with you, Maybeline, I wouldn't do this." He kissed me. "That means you're my friend and I could never fake that."

"That means I'm your friend?" I brushed a tear out of my eye.

"Yes," he said. "Here, let me grab you something for your…your…whatever." He motioned to his eyes as he grabbed some paper towels. "Your makeup, that's what it is." He rubbed them under my eyes.

"Facetus?" I barely whispered.

"What?" He lowered the paper towel from my face.

"Is your name, like, vampiran or something? Because it's really hard to say. Are all your names like that?"

He paused, thinking. "My name is Latin," he said. "And yes, many other vampires have Latin names too. Hazley is young enough she has a more modern name."

"So, Hazley's one too?"

"Yes. Yes, she is."

"Facetus? Why do you all have Latin names?"

"We used to speak Latin," he said. "But that's not spoken anymore, so now we speak English."

"So, your first language is Latin?"

"It's my first human language," he replied, "but not my first language. Vampires have their own way of communicating, just like any other animal."

"I guess that's true." I hadn't really thought that much about other animals communicating before. "So, what's your name in...vampire-talk?" I asked him.

"We don't have names," he said.

"Then, how do you know who you're talking to?"

"I mean, we don't have individual titles," he said.

"Good thing you had to become human," I said, "or else, what would I call you?"

He nodded. "I suppose that's true."

I looked around the room. I was feeling much better now. I wondered when we would go back to the dance room. I was examining the white tiled wall when all of a sudden, I was startled by a deep, rough, incoherent voice that I could only imagine the monster under my bed had.

"What was that!" I asked in panic.

"That was what my father called me," Facetus laughed.

"Oh," I sighed in relief.

"Are you ready to go back out?" he asked me.

"Yeah," I said.

Chapter 38

There wasn't anybody in the hallway when we came out to my relief. Facetus held the ballroom door open for me.

"Oh, honey, there you are!" my mom greeted me. "I've been looking all over for you!" She acknowledged Facetus. "Ooh, and it looks like you and your friend 'ran into each other' here?" She winked at me.

"Mom," I said.

"Oh, I'm just teasing you." She giggled. "Obviously you didn't actually *plan* to meet here." She winked again.

I gave her that shut-up-or-die look.

She ignored me and turned her attention to Facetus. "So, hon, how've you been? I haven't seen you since you were such a gentleman and brought my poor daughter to see me on that rainy day."

"I'm feeling all right," he said. "How are you?"

"Oh, I'm doing just fine. Come over here. You've got to try some of my famous homemade chip dip!"

"But this is the first time you've made it!" I said. "How can it be famous?"

"Oh, it will be, sweetheart, it will be," my mom told

me. She said to Facetus, "I'm going to get a patent for it and everything! We're going to have magazines, newspapers, a television crew come in and interview my dip. It's going to be huge, I tell you!"

Facetus munched on a chip slathered in dip slowly as he watched my mother with curiosity.

"So? What do you think of Margret D. Chevy's world-famous taste-tastic, taster-rific, tasteful delight of tasty—"

"O.K., Mom!" I said.

"I wasn't finished," she said. She turned back to Facetus. "Where was I? Oh yes. Delightful tastiness, taste-mazing crew of tast—"

"You did a good job, Mrs. Chevy," Facetus said.

"Oh no, it's just Miss," she said. Facetus nodded. "All right, we need to get a photo of you two!" she said, pulling out her phone. Facetus walked over to me and my mom positioned her camera. "Hold on," she said, lowering her phone. "You need to be closer together." She positioned the camera again. We each took a step closer. "Closer," she said. We moved closer. "Closer, closer." And still, we continued to edge toward the other. "Closer—"

"Mom, our shoulders are touching!" I said when I

thought it'd be impossible to get any *closer!*

"Come on," she said, "act like you actually like each other."

I gave my mom a look. Facetus threw his arm around me and leaned his head against my shoulder.

"Perfect!" my mom said. "Three…two…. Come on, Maybeline, *smile."*

I groaned and tried not to look like I was about to strangle somebody.

"There!" my mom said, finally taking the photo. "Oh, it's just perfect!" She showed us the picture.

"Ew, is that what I really look like?" I said. But Mom was right; it *was* a pretty decent shot. Unless someone knew, they would probably think my lack of cheer would be because the photo was quick and I didn't realize it was being taken until it was being taken. Facetus had on his charming smile and his golden eyes were the eye-catcher of the entire picture. It was odd to see him in dress-up clothes. It was odd to see *me* in dress-up clothes.

"You know, the blue of your dress really brings out the blue of your eyes," Facetus said. Huh, he was right.

"This one's going in the album!" my mom said,

putting her phone away.

"'In the album'?" I said. "But Mom, isn't everything digital now?"

"Oh, I'll find a way, sweetums. I will find a way," she said. "Bye. Oh, you two are just so cute!"

"You didn't by any chance learn ways to know what a person doesn't straight-forwardly say in school, did you?" I asked as she walked away.

"No," he said. I sighed in relief. "But," he continued, "through my experience of understanding human emotion, I'd say she thinks we're dating."

"Of course you do," I said.

"I mean, that *could* be incorrect," he said.

"No, you're correct," I said. *"Perfectly* correct."

"So, what else do you do at this little…whatever?" He motioned across the whole room.

"I don't know," I shrugged. "I guess, just have fun? Or at least, try to?"

"So…." I looked around. There didn't appear to be anyone in earshot. "You kiss your friends, right?"

"Yes," Facetus replied.

"What do you do with your girlfriends?" I asked.

"Um, mate?" he said.

"That's it?"

He shrugged. "Nothing else I can think of."

"Well, don't you try to get to know them first?"

He shrugged again. "I guess, whatever happens in the minutes leading up to it."

"That's weird."

"It's called wild."

"Do they get jealous when you hang out with other girls?"

"No. Why would they?"

"Well, I mean, because it's *other girls.*"

"So what? I'm not allowed to have any friends?"

"Well, no, but I mean, humans, if they're a girl, usually all their friends are girls and then they have a boyfriend. Same with boys. Boy friends and one girlfriend."

"Vampires are very territorial creatures," he said. "If you're a boy, all your friends are girls. If you're a girl, all your friends are boys. And besides, you're likely never going to interact with your mate again in your life unless they're a friend, so…."

"So Hazley probably doesn't like me," I said.

"No, Hazley likes you," he said.

"But I thought girls don't like girls," I said. "Or is it because I'm human?"

"No, species doesn't really matter," he said. "Hazley has…a *different* past than most people and I'm the only person she trusts, so if I say you're my friend, then you're her friend."

"Wow," I said. "But why are you the only person she trusts?"

He paused. "That's a very complicated answer, Maybeline."

"Is she a child too?" I asked. "Like me?"

"Yes. Yes, she is," he said very solemnly, almost sadly.

Chapter 39

It wasn't long after that the gathering came to an end and everyone began departing. Because my mom was a part of the committee this year, she had to stay behind and help clean up, which meant I had to stay behind because she was the one who had brought me here and the one who would be taking me home.

It wasn't all bad waiting though. Before the music was officially turned off, Facetus taught me a few more dance steps. We were the last ones on the dance floor, and I tried to ignore my mother, who was obviously very happy about that fact.

When the music was turned off, Facetus leaned over to kiss me, remembered something, and hugged me instead. "Thank you, Maybie," he whispered in my ear.

"Thank me?" I said. "You were the one who taught me."

"Yes, but I had so much fun," he said as we walked back over to where my mom, one of the people clearing the refreshments table, was.

"You really like dancing?" I asked.

"My favorite human creation is timeless," he

replied.

"Oh, you two looked so beautiful dancing together!" my mom said as we reached her. "Hey, hon, I'm sorry. This is taking longer than I thought. I won't be able to take you home until later."

"It's all right, Mom," I said. "I don't mind waiting."

"I could take you home if you like," Facetus offered. My mom's face lit up.

Oh no.

"Oh yes, that will perfect!" she said. "And then you two can spend some quality time together!"

"Mom." I couldn't believe she was taking it *this* far.

"Oh, I kno—" She started giggling. She was still giggling when we left the ballroom. I couldn't hear her anymore by the time we reached the exit for the building itself, but I wouldn't be surprised if she still was. Imagine what her fellow volunteers thought of her *now*.

Apparently he had walked here, so I walked with Facetus back to my apartment. It was really quiet since I didn't know what to talk about. I don't think Facetus knew either. We had already talked about so much in such a short amount of time.

"Man, I'm hungry," I finally broke the silence. Wait.

Maybe I shouldn't have said that….

Facetus didn't say anything.

After a few more silent moments, I said, "How can you be friends with me?"

"What do you mean?" he replied. He continued to look forward.

"I mean, you're predator, I'm prey. Don't you get it? How can you be friends with something you eat?"

"How can the farm kid have a pet pig?" he said. "You have a pet, Maybeline. Don't you understand?"

"No, not really," I said. "I don't eat dogs."

"I know you don't, but it's…. They're special to you. Even though they're not the same species, you still love and care for them…. I'm sorry, I'm supposed to say 'like,' aren't I?"

"No no, it's fine," I said. "I get what you mean." I looked back at him. He was still staring straight ahead. "Are you O.K.?" I asked. I was afraid I'd done something wrong.

"Yes, I'm fine," he said. He was watching the ground now. "How are you?"

"I'm all right…," I said. "But are you sure? You haven't said much and you're watching the ground."

He looked up and slowly turned to me. I couldn't

read his expression. After a moment, he let his eyelids drop and he continued to watch the ground.

We soon reached my apartment, which hadn't been far from the dance.

"Aren't you going to go home?" I asked as I opened the door to the complex.

He simply stared at me. "I don't want to go home," he eventually said.

"O.K...," I said, stepping inside.

"Do you want me to leave?" He had that pleading look in his golden eyes again. He reminded me of a puppy begging for something. Well, that's what he was: an animal.

"Of course she wants you to leave, you stinking rat!" We were both startled by the old man.

I started to say, "Mr. Rockwell—"

"And now you're talking to chairs?" Ms. Fellers screeched. "You're starting to lose it, Frank!"

"I am not losing it! There's two people standing right there!" he yelled back.

While the elderly continued their bickering, I motioned to Facetus to follow me up the stairs.

"Do you want me to leave?" he asked again when we reached the third floor. "Do you want me to go? I'll go if you tell me to, or maybe you want me to leave forever or—"

"Facetus! No, it's O.K." I smiled at him. "You can stay if you want."

"Yes, but what do *you* want? For me to go?"

"Why are you freaking out?"

"I'm not freaking out! Are you freaking out? 'Cause I'm not freak—"

"Facetus, calm down! Tell me what's wrong. Please."

He stared at the floor. We were standing in front of my apartment now.

"Facetus?" I asked softly.

His head snapped up. "You hate me, don't you? You hate me because of what I am and you want me to go!"

"No, Facetus, I—"

"No! Don't try to lie to me, no! I know it. You can't deny it." He turned to go.

"Facetus, stop!" I said in my most authoritative voice.

He stopped dead in his tracks.

Works every time.

Chapter 40

In my experience as a dog owner, I've learned that you need to be gentle with animals, but sometimes you need to be tough. Facetus was no excuse.

"Turn around," I said. He hesitated. *"Turn…around."* He slowly turned to face me, his head lowered. "Look at me," I said. *"Look at me."* He slowly raised his head. But before I could say anything more, my apartment door swung open.

"What? What is it?" Marcie raced to me. "What did he do to you? What?" She turned to Facetus. "Stay back, you stinking rat! I got pepper spray and I'm not afraid to use it!" She held up a can. "What did he do? Tell me, tell me quick. What did he do?" she said to me, still looking at Facetus.

"He—he didn't do anything to me, Marcie," I said.

"Well, I heard yelling, so it was obviously something."

"No, no, Marcie, it was…. He didn't do anything, we were—"

"What? What were you doing?"

"We were…. We had a disagreement on something."

"Is all of this true?" Marcie sternly asked Facetus. He looked distressed. I would be too if my friend had used her I'm-the-boss voice and then her roommate had come on the scene yielding a can of pepper spray. Actually, I'd be downright confused, but he was already upset, so….

"*Is it* true?" Marcie asked again. Facetus nodded slowly. "All right," she said, lowering her hand. "If you need me, I'll be indulging in pancakes." She walked back into the apartment.

"Ooh, pancakes?" I exclaimed, starting to follow her. I stopped and backed up a few paces. "Come on, Facetus," I said. He didn't move. "Come on. You're a good boy." I patted him on the head. "I'll give you a treat when we get inside."

He looked less upset and more are you kidding me. Well, it's still progress.

"Come on, please?" I said. "I want you to come. I really do. *Please?*" I stared up into his eyes. He blinked twice, the rest of him unmoving. I smiled at him. He quickly broke the eye contact.

"I will do as you say," he said.

"I just want to enjoy some time with my friend," I said. "It's as simple as that. No I say or you say. Just…

fun. And happiness."

He seemed puzzled for a moment. Then he outburst, "You're trying to trick me!"

"What? No, I—"

"I see right through it!"

"Facetus—"

"I see what you're trying to do to me!"

"Facetus—"

"Don't think nobody's ever tried it before!"

"Tried what? Facetus—" My words stopped coming out. I was still very afraid of this side of Facetus.

His veins popped out of his throat and his eyes were completely black. His nose reminded me of a bird's beak as it became narrower and arched slightly downward. This was the Facetus who'd attacked Robert....

I felt myself shake.

"I'm leaving!" he said in a deep voice. And a split second later, he was out of sight.

"Everything all right out there?" I heard Marcie cautiously say.

I shakily nodded.

She came out into the hallway. "Are *you* all right?" she asked. "Where's what's-his-face? What happened?"

"Yeah," was all I could make out. Marcie guided me into the apartment. I was starving but I'd lost my appetite. I picked at the pancakes I was desiring to consume but had no willpower to do so. I eventually got a pancake and 2/3 eaten, but it took me a few hours. I needed to cry but my eyes couldn't wet. I needed to scream but my voice was broken.

I was scared to death of him.

And I had every right to be.

His words continued to echo through my head as the day passed. What was wrong with him? Why did he think I was trying to trick him—and *what* did he think I was trying to trick him into? What about the "don't think nobody's ever tried it before" part? Do people generally try to trick Facetus? And if so, why?

The more I thought about it, the more confused I became. When I thought I couldn't take it anymore, I suddenly remembered something.

I remembered this morning, when Facetus had told me that he hadn't killed anyone. Whew. So I was all worked up over nothing! That's a relief! Yes, Facetus doesn't kill anyone, Facetus…Facetus…Facetus…. I remembered something else.

I'm not killing…everybody.
Of course. Not *everybody.*
Hey, what happened to your hand?
Oh, it—it's nothing.
His cuts.
What? What happened?
In an attack last night, it broke a decoration or something in the person's house, and they found its blood on some of the broken pieces.
It was right in front of me the whole time.
You won't get there until after dark. That's when the attacks happen.
The police have no idea when they're happening.
Tulsa said they attack at night.
I've been keeping up on the news and they haven't said anything about that.
How could I have been so oblivious?
I will tear him apart!
No, Facetus, no!
Oh. My. God.

Chapter 41

"Marcie!" I screamed, and ran to the door to make sure it was locked. Yes.

"What? What is it?" Marcie asked, coming to me.

"O.K., so…." I ran to check all the windows. Marcie followed.

"What? Maybeline, what's going on?"

"So, um…." I didn't know how to tell her. "So, um, well, what if—what if vampires and stuff—you know, from the movies—were real? So—"

"Maybeline, you're all worked up about fictional creatures?"

"Well, so…." How do I put this? "You know how Facetus and I sort of, um—"

"Got into a fight?"

"Yeah." I sat on the couch, as I was satisfied with the locks. "Well, I was thinking about this vampire movie, and well, the main character doesn't know whether she should trust him or not—the vampire. Do you think she should trust him?"

"What does this have to do with you and what's-his-face?"

"It doesn't, I'm just…trying to think of something

else," I said.

"O.K....," Marcie said. "And what vampire movie was this?"

"Um, I don't know what it's called," I said. "They were showing it at the dance and I didn't get to see the end of it, so...well, I don't know if she trusts him or not."

"They were showing a movie at the dance?" Marcie asked. "Wow, they've really upped their game."

"Yeah...." Hopefully she would forget about it.

"So what? Are they in a relationship or something and she finds out what he is one way or another?"

"Um, yes," I said. I really wasn't quite sure how I felt about Facetus at this point. "Yes, they are and, um, well, there's been a lot of strange disappearances of... bodies drained of blood"—better make this sound practical—"and all—"

"Wait, how do they know if they're drained of blood if they have disappeared?"

"Um...I don't know. I think it was a cheap film. Anyway, all the signs of the attacks point to him, but he's such a nice person, so...."

"Well, I say don't trust him then," Marcie said. "The facts point to him, and some people are really good at playing pretend. Always trust the facts, Maybeline, always trust the facts."

I was afraid she was going to say that.

Then came a strange tapping sound at the door. Marcie started to get up. I motioned for her to get back down. She looked at me in question. The tapping continued. Then we heard a female voice. It wasn't saying any words though—at least, not that we could make out. Marcie cautiously made her way to the door. I didn't try to stop her this time as I watched with suspense. She slowly opened the door a crack. Satisfied with what she saw, she let it swing all the way open.

"Hello," Marcie said.

Hazley made more noise before she finally made out words. "H-h-hello."

"Hazley, are you all right?" I asked carefully, not wanting to let my guard down. The girl didn't look well, her wavy blond locks disheveled and partly in her face.

"I...I...." She didn't seem to know what to say.

"Why don't you come in?" Marcie offered.

Hazley cautiously stepped in, making careful glances left and right as she proceeded into our

apartment. I wondered why she seemed so scared....
Should I even wonder anymore? No, she looked
worse today.

"Hazley, are you all right?" I asked again, a little
more concerned this time.

She looked at me with worried blue eyes. "I...I...
why...why...why Facetus mad?"

"I don't kno—"

"He no talk to me!" she said. "He mad, mad. I no
know why."

"I don't know either," I said. "He said he thinks I
tricked him."

"You trick him?" She seemed even more upset.

"No, I didn't," I said. "He *thinks* I tricked him."

She seemed confused by this. Kind of like how
Facetus had when I'd asked him to come in with
me....

"I did not trick him, Hazley," I said. "Have people
tricked him before?"

She got very silent and still. "Have they?" I asked
again, quite intrigued.

She stared at me with an expression that told me
the answer was yes.

"Who's tricked him?" I asked. "Why? How?"

"She say she angel," Hazley said at last.

"What?" I didn't quite understand.

"She trick him," she said. "She say she angel, but she demon."

"Who?" I was intrigued. I could tell Marcie was too. Hazley didn't answer.

"Who, Hazley?" Eventually, I dared to say, "The people he's killed?" Marcie and Hazley both looked at me, wide eyed.

"The people he's *killed?*" Marcie exclaimed.

Hazley looked at me with question. "How you…?"

"Are those the people, Hazley?" I asked, feeling a lump in my throat. If the answer *was* yes, I would be in a lot of trouble. "Are those the people he's killed? The ones who trick him?"

"No," she said. "He no kill she. She alpha!"

"'Alpha'?" Marcie questioned.

"Yes." Hazley nodded. "She alpha. He no can kill her!"

"So, it's just one person?" I asked. "Someone like you and Facetus?"

She didn't answer.

"Why does he kill all those people?" Better ask as many questions as I can while Hazley was still here and I was still brave.

"Hold on, *what?*" Marcie asked. "Maybeline, what's going on? Are you saying that he's a murderer?"

"Well, why does he?" I said to Hazley. "Doesn't he know it's wrong to do? I mean, every day, farm people are showing up dea—"

"No!" Hazley said suddenly. "No, Facetus no do that!"

"What do you mea—"

"Facetus angel! Contrarietas demon!"

"What?" I don't think I caught all of that.

She stared at me like a child who'd accidentally told his mother he'd eaten all the cookies.

"I go find Facetus," she said. And with that, she abruptly turned and left, faster than I could protest.

"Maybeline," Marcie said quietly after a minute, "is he…does he…*kill* people? Is that why you were fighting?"

"Well, I—"

"You can't see him anymore! No, you stay as far away from him as possible!" She was speaking quite loudly now. "We got to do something, Maybeline. He's a murderer. We've got to turn him in to the police!"

"Marcie, he's not the kind of murderer you thin—"

"We need to tell them so they can take care of this!"

"Yes, but they won't be able to catch him!" He would kill them before they even knew he was there. Oh god, how do I get out of this mess?

Chapter 42

"Maybeline, how long have you known about this?" Marcie asked as she paced the room.

"I don't want to talk a—"

"Maybeline!" She stopped pacing. "How long have you been keeping this a secret from me? How long?"

"Well, you see, I haven't *exactly* been—"

"When did you find out?"

"Just this morning, really. Well…just last night. But I didn't know for sure!"

"Oh, Maybeline, this is really bad! Don't you know how bad this is?"

"Yes, I do, Marcie." I really did.

"I don't—I don't even know what to do about this or what to even think, I—" She put her head in her hands. I don't think I'd ever seen her so upset before. "I just—I need to lie down—No, I need to call the police—No—*Ah!*" she groaned.

"Marcie, you need to relax," I said. "You're not thinking right right now, so go lie down, and we can mess with this later—"

"But we need to call the police!"

"I'll take care of it," I said. Well, there was a

commitment I wasn't willing to do. "Go rest."

She reluctantly went off to the hall. She stopped. "What if—"

"Go. I will take care of it, see?" I dug out my phone. "Go. Clear your mind."

"Don't forget to—"

"I know everything I'm going to say, Marcie."

"Well, maybe I should—"

"Hey, you take a psychology class, right? Isn't stress bad for the brain?"

"Yes, but—"

"And besides, I know more about it than you do. *Much* more." I got her there. She didn't know what else to say. "Go," I beckoned again. "And close your door so I'm not disturbing you," I added.

Great, how am I going to do this? I asked myself as soon as she'd gone. I stared at my phone. I couldn't do it. I couldn't guide those people into a trap…but then Facetus would keep killing people. I sighed aloud. I would go to the police station and hopefully make them understand.

I quietly tiptoed out the door and went down the stairs. Luckily, my noise-free appearance kept Mr. Rockwell and Ms. Fellers from noticing me. I walked out into the late-afternoon air. I glanced carefully around. No one in sight. I didn't want to risk Facetus or Hazley seeing me. I got in my car and drove to the station.

I parked the car and got out. The wind was very light and it was eerily quiet out. Spooky. Perfect for the climax of a horror movie. I tried to shake the feeling as I approached the building.

About halfway to the door, I thought I heard a strange noise behind me. I turned around but didn't see anything. *Must have been an animal,* I thought. I turned back around and nearly had the life scared out of me.

"Where you going?" he skeptically asked.

I started shivering.

"Where you going, Maybeline?" He removed his sunglasses, revealing his amber eyes.

"I was just—just—"

"You weren't going to the police station, were you?" He looked at the tall building. He turned back to me. "Is that drunken red-haired one after you again?"

"No, I, uh, I was just—"

"So, what would you need to be at the police station for?"

"I-I—" I could run, but he was close enough to me that he could grab me on a dime. I wouldn't get anywhere that way. I might also anger him that way too.

"It wouldn't be…to tell them something…that you've recently learned…would it?" There was no fear or concern at all in his voice. In fact, his tone was spine-tinglingly dark.

"I—"

"'Cause that wouldn't be smart."

I couldn't take it anymore.

I turned and took maybe two steps to my car before he caught me. "No, let me go!" I cried. He covered my mouth with his hand.

"Come on, Maybie. Let's go somewhere together," he said. I could feel his moist breath on the back of my neck.

Chapter 43

I struggled against his grip, but it was no use. His arm was like steel; I didn't even stand a chance in escaping. He was leading me away from the building.

I was surprised that our path ended at my car.

His arm of steel dropped from my torso and retrieved the car key from my pocket. He unlocked the doors and then forced me into the passenger seat. He slammed the door and walked around to the driver side. I tried to open my door, but it was locked. I would try yelling. "Hel—" Facetus threw his hand over my mouth, pressing my head against the back of the seat in the process, as he closed the driver-side door.

I desperately tried to pry his hand off my face and let my pain show in my eyes as much as possible. He barely looked at me though.

I could feel something sharp against my cheek. I realized he still had the key in that hand. Thankfully, the metal ring was just dangling from one of his fingers, and so the actual key wasn't between my face and his hand.

I was twisting my head, trying to loosen his grip, when I caught sight of him staring at me. I couldn't help pausing in shock. He still looked human, but the way his eyes burned into me was unsettling. No, it was downright horrific.

"You don't scream, *understand?*" he growled to me. I did my best to nod. He started to loosen his grip on my jaw, but just as I was starting to breathe comfortably again, he quickly tightened around it again. If he hadn't been hindering it, I would have gasped in surprise. He continued to stare at me.

After a long disturbing moment, he slowly let his hand fall from my face and, still watching me, started the car. If I hadn't been so afraid, I would've tried screaming for help again. Maybe he had known that.

Another minute passed, and he finally, slowly, turned his eyes away from me. He let out a long breath and started the car forward. I wondered where he was going to take me. Odd, though, he drove rather slowly. *Maybe he isn't very experienced in driving cars,* I thought.

"You know, Marcie's going to be worried about me," I mumbled, looking down at my hands. Facetus didn't say anything. I watched a teardrop fall onto my thumb. It was the end of my life, I knew it.

And soon, I was bawling. What made it worse was

that Facetus didn't pay any attention to me, like he doesn't have any care when it comes to human pain. Of course he doesn't; he *causes* it.

I felt the car slowly roll to a stop. I looked up. We were stopped at an intersection, but there were no other cars. I looked at Facetus. He was staring straight ahead.

I wiped the tears from my face and watched him. He was very unmoving and still. *Is this it?* I thought. *Is he preparing to finish me right now? Or perhaps he is acting calm so that I'll come closer to him, or start trusting and be unsuspecting of him, or both?* The anticipation was killing me. Bad choice of words....

He looked at me.

It was so sudden that I jumped and a gasp got caught in my throat.

He looked back to the road.

I could feel my heart pounding in my chest. His knuckles were white on the steering wheel. He was still mad at me. And for what, I didn't know.

"Why are you mad at me?" My words were so quiet I barely even heard my own voice. I wasn't sure if Facetus had heard me or not; he continued to stare straight ahead. "Please tell me," my voice broke, and I

felt a few more tears trickle down my face.
"Facetus...."

He slowly turned to me.

"Please tell me," I repeated my plead.

He stared at me in the silence. I waited for his answer, but it never came. He looked back at the road.

"Face—*ahh!*" I screamed.

The car gunned forward. I looked at my arm. There were red stinging lines across it.

I couldn't believe he'd done that. I knew what he was, but I still couldn't believe he'd done that. I looked at him in shock. He was watching the road as if nothing had happened. I looked back down at my arm. The claw marks were huge. I wondered about what I could use to blot the blood.

There was no way I was going to try to talk to Facetus now. As if I hadn't been afraid before....

I had no idea what I could use about the blood, so I just sat there and hoped it would stop soon. I was looking down for most of the car ride. When I did look up, all I could see was countryside. *Countryside.*

I dared to look at the monster again. Same as he'd been last time I'd looked at him. He pulled the car to the side of the road. He got out and walked around to my side. I didn't hesitate when he opened my door. I quickly got out and stood a couple feet away from him, waiting for him to tell me what to do.

He shut my door and looked at me. "Come," he said. I followed him down the road. I was itching to ask where we were going, but after what'd happened last time, I found my tongue didn't work.

I looked around. There weren't any cars or people in sight. Great. The perfect environment for Facetus to kill me. I never thought it'd end this way. I hadn't really thought about it before, but I always figured I'd peacefully pass in the presence of my children or in a nursing home, not brutally murdered by a monster.

Facetus stopped walking.

Chapter 44

I held my breath as I watched him. He turned to face me. "Come on," he said. When I hesitated, he growled, *"Come on!"* and yanked me along with him.

I shrieked with pain and somehow wiggled out of his grasp. I looked down at my arm. He'd grabbed me right where he'd previously scratched me earlier. He didn't make any more cuts, but I could see faded red marks where he'd held me. I quickly glanced up. I didn't want to risk looking away from him for too long.

He had a puzzled expression on his face. I held my breath, watching him closely. He stared at me for another moment before leading me off the gravel road and into an empty field. I was relieved he guided me by my back instead of my arm this time.

I was careful where I stepped—which wasn't very easy—as Facetus led me farther into the weeds. I remembered my dad telling me to stay out of places like this—for here dwelled snakes and ticks and other creepy things you don't want to run into. I wasn't wearing pants of any sort—I still had on the dress my mom had made me wear—so the brambles scraped my legs as I passed. Facetus, however, had on his normal shirt and jeans he's worn every day since I've met him.

At the end of the field was a sea of trees. When I struggled to get over the barrier of dead branches and weeds dividing the field from the trees, Facetus effortlessly scooped me up and over it.

Every second as we descended farther into the woods, I expected him to turn around and attack me, but he didn't. We were getting so deep into the forest, the thickness blocked out the setting sun and it was almost completely dark. Eerily dark.

Facetus disappeared from my sight.

Frantically, I glanced around but I couldn't find him.

"Come on!"

His voice startled me. I looked up. He had ascended on to a rock formation high above ground. I cautiously examined the structure, trying to find something sturdy to hang on to.

"Come on, Maybeline!" he hollered again. I could tell he was getting impatient.

I tried to quicken my search and tested a few ledges. They all seemed firm, but they weren't very big and I didn't think I could hang on to them.

I heard Facetus heave a huge annoyed sigh from

above. I tried harder. I heard a *thump* next to me and I jumped in surprise. He had dropped down from the flat plateau he had been standing on, and he looked pissed. "Come on," he said in a tone calmer than his expression.

He stood in the small space between me and the rock, his back to me. He bent down and grabbed my arms from behind, securing them around his shoulders and neck. "Hang on," he said, and jumped.

It happened so fast, I shrieked and clung to him as tight as I could. He leaped from ledge to ledge, plateau to plateau, springing higher than I'd ever known a human to do, his claws cutting through the rock and helping him to ascend higher.

I wondered how high this thing was, and I was beginning to wonder if it was a mountain. We were running out of ledges and plateaus. Facetus still leaped high enough to reach the next though.

He slipped.

And I screamed. The jolt had caused me to loosen my grip on him, and now I was dangling for dear life. His claws slid and he repositioned one, probably trying to get a better grip. But when his shoulder moved, my arm slipped and I screamed again. My reflexes acting fast, I miraculously was able to grab his middle. Both his legs were dangling too, and I wrapped mine around one of his, trying to feel more secure. It didn't help much though. My mind and heart were still racing.

My one hand still on his shoulder struggled to hang on as he climbed higher, sinking his claws into the rock and then pulling them out again to ascend. He reached the plateau and bent his arms, pulling him and me higher. He clung farther across the plateau, and eventually pulled us both completely up.

"Get off me," he said. I obeyed. He rose to his feet. He looked exhausted. I was too, and I wasn't even the one climbing.

He walked across the plateau—this one was much bigger than the other ones we'd been on—and looked out across everything below. I tiptoed up to have a look for myself. We were higher up than I think I'd ever been in my life, and yet there was still lots of mountain ahead of us. The wind whipped through my hair. I could see practically all of New York from up here. If I hadn't been so afraid, I'd have been *amazed.*

I looked at Facetus. He was staring out into the open. I couldn't tell if he was human or not; it was too dark to tell. I wondered why we'd—well, *he'd*—climbed up this much rock. *What if he was going to push me off the ledge?*

I took a step back at that thought.

"Facetus?"

I turned around. I couldn't see her, but I recognized that voice as Hazley's.

"Come here, baby girl," I heard him say. I saw his silhouette engulf hers, and he kissed her. "Where's Contrarietas?" he asked, still holding her.

"He left," she said.

"Are you O.K.?" he asked after a pause.

I didn't hear her say anything in response. In fact, everything was silent in the minutes that passed. I looked back at New York from a distance. It was getting darker and much harder to see anything, but at least I had that faint glow of city lights.

"We have to go," I heard Facetus break the steady silence.

I heard what sounded like a kiss, and then I heard Hazley say, "May...ween?"

"Maybeline's going to stay here," Facetus said.

"Wait, *what?*" I panicked. "You're going to leave me up here?" This was even worse. I was going to *starve*.

"I'll come bac—"

"No no no no no no no no. No," I interrupted him. Oops, that probably wasn't smart….

"Maybeline, I'm not going to lea—"

"No. No, you can't do that! No!" I knew I should've kept quiet, but I was freaking out and having trouble controlling my actions. "No. No, Facetus, don't leave me here. Kill me, kill me now!" No matter how much he would tear me apart, I was certain it would be better than dying of hunger.

There was silence from both of the vampires, which scared me even more because I could no longer see them.

"You want die?" I eventually heard Hazley say. *Oh no, had it come off to them like that? I didn't want that!*

"No!" I frantically said. "I mean, I just meant—I…I…it would be better to die fast than slow!" I finally spit out.

Silence.

Oh no oh no oh no….

"Contrarietas will kill her," Hazley said.

"I know," Facetus said.

Wait, *what?*

"Who's Conta—Who—who's that?" I shrieked with

fear.

Chapter 45

"Who?" I asked again.

Facetus started to say, "Contrariet—"

"Contrarietas what?" I heard a third voice now. I hadn't thought it was possible for me to lose it any more than I already was, but I somehow found a way. "Ooh, what's this?" the voice continued. "A treat for me? Oh, Facetus, you shouldn't have! She looks just *perfect.*" The voice had eerily dropped from cheerily thankful to mortifyingly dark. I took a step back in fear.

"Do you have a name, little one?" The cheery voice became louder. *"Oh,"* she laughed. "But that won't matter anyway because I'm still going to kill you." I edged back a little farther. "Oh, Facetus, I forgive you for being late. She just looks so *tasty.*" The voice was right in front of me now. I jumped back in fright and landed on…nothing. *Nothing!*

I shrieked as the cold wind blew my hair and butterflies started dancing—no, *fighting*—in my stomach. I felt like it was never going to end. Couldn't death come quickly instead of drawn out in painful suspension?

All of a sudden, I felt something close around my

torso. Then my head jolted forward and my hair fell around my face. I struggled to catch my breath as I tried to figure out what had happened—which didn't take long....

"Maybeline!" The thing that had grabbed me dropped me to my feet. "Why do you have to be so stupid!" A pair of hands grabbed my wrists and shook me as their person's voice yelled in my face. "And so oblivious and—and—" The voice struggled to go on. "Swear you will never do that again you foolish, foolish girl!" I realized the voice belonged to Facetus. I don't think I'd ever heard him yell—like, truly yell—before. That's when I also realized I was sobbing. Facetus groaned. "You ought to be ashamed of your foolishness and be punished greatly for your stupidity, I...."

"Ugh, come *on,* Facetus!" I heard Contrarietas say. At that same moment I felt someone yank me—by my uninjured arm, luckily—away from Facetus. "You should've just let her die," I heard Contrarietas's voice say by my ear. "Can't you walk any faster, you stupid old human? Come, let's teach you a thing or two."

All through the trek in the forest, Contrarietas showed no aid to my blindness as I tripped over things and ran into stuff; she just kept yanking me along. I remembered Hazley saying Facetus was an angel and someone else was a demon. Could she have been referring to the fact that Facetus showed much more mercy than Contrarietas? And I could only imagine the awful things he had done to me were butterflies and rainbows compared to what she might.

After more unpleasant moments of being towed—or rather dragged—through a thick forest, I spotted light up ahead. I wondered where it was coming from.

We stopped.

Chapter 46

"Hazley, stay here and make sure the human doesn't wander off," Contrarietas said. Then she and Facetus both went off somewhere and out of my sight.

I looked around. I tried my best to peer through the trees to see where the light was coming from.

When my eyes adjusted, I could see porches and huge yards. The lights were coming from outside lights on people's houses.

In the dim light, something small and lean caught my eye. It crept along the plain cautiously, and when it got closer to one of the light sources, I could see it was the same color as the light projected onto it.

What was it?

I watched it cautiously even though I was probably safe from it in the trees. It crouched down and peered around the corner of the house.

I had a disturbing thought. What if *this* was the thing attacking people and *not* the vampires, and that Facetus had been telling the truth?

I shivered as I watched it. As if it had heard me, its head immediately turned in my direction and its light, but rich, brown eyes stared at me. The eyes seemed so familiar, but I couldn't place them. Familiar or not, they frightened me, and I began to question the security of my spot behind the trees.

It turned away from me after a moment and continued on its way. *It was a fox, that's what it was,* I realized. But I had never known a fox to be custard in color....

After a few feet of travel, the fox stopped. And it did the strangest thing. It began jumping up and down, stomping its feet on the ground. Weren't foxes supposed to be quiet?

Then it started vocalizing, producing yowls and other strange animal noises. I saw a figure run around the side of the house. He was carrying a flashlight. When he came closer to the porch light, I could see he was a policeman. Just before he reached the animal, it scurried away. The officer hurried after it as it ran across the plain.

As it neared more houses, more policemen took notice of it, and soon it had a pack of officers after it.

They ended up circling it, shining their lights down on it. It covered its eyes with its paws. The police looked at one another. Then, still crouched down, the fox waved its bushy golden tail, placing its front legs in front of it, and sprang off the ground. The policemen watched in awe as it soared over them and trampled somewhere into the forest—not near me, luckily, but I was still nervous.

It was all silent for a moment and the policemen all returned to their posts. Suddenly, I heard footsteps.

I turned, trying to pinpoint where they were coming from, so anxious I thought I might faint. A figure emerged from the trees, and I jumped back in fright, running into a tree and some shrubbery. The person was out of breath.

"How are you doing, Hazley?" I heard Facetus say breathlessly.

She didn't answer. During the silence, I saw Facetus put his arm around Hazley's shoulders. I wondered if that was their form of hugging, as I remembered Facetus saying they don't hug. After a moment, Facetus said, "Come on. Bring Maybeline."

And so, I followed him and Hazley down the border of trees, and waited with a house in front of us. I wasn't sure what we were waiting for, but when the policeman walked to the front, they both scurried across the yard to the porch. They looked back, their silhouettes eerie against the porch light. They were staring at *me.*

I cautiously took a step forward. Facetus frantically waved his arms. I stopped and backed up, but that only made it worse. He raced back to the trees and pulled me to the porch—so fast I had to do a double take. They both quickly ushered me inside. I wondered what we were doing here.

I saw a flicker of light in the corner of my eye. The light was coming from upstairs, and the most deformed shadow I'd ever seen was descending down.

I quickly hid behind Facetus. I was still terrified of him, but right now he seemed much safer than what I might meet across the room.

I heard the figure's footsteps as it continued down the stairs and came closer to us. Then all was silent. I noticed Facetus shift a little.

Then I felt a hand on my upper back. I gasped in surprise. The person guided me gently through the quiet dark house, so I could only assume it was Facetus. Contrarietas would be painful. Where was she anyway?

Facetus—or whoever it was—put pressure down on my shoulder, so I slowly went to my knees. I had no clue what the three—oh god, what if there were *more*—vampires would do to me, but I decided it would be best to do whatever they asked me to—or at least, what I *thought* they asked.

"You stay here," I heard Facetus's voice say in the dark. I wasn't sure if he could see me, but I nodded anyway. "Would it be more comfortable if you slid over there so you could lean against the flat part of the counter?" I glanced around in the dark but I still couldn't see anything. "I forgot you can't see in the dark," he said. He guided me a bit across the floor, and I leaned back against something hard. It felt good to rest even though I was still anxious and worried. "I'll be back."

"Facetus...," I began softly. I wanted to ask him while he was still calm, but I had no idea what would flip his violence switch. "What...?" Was he still there? All I heard was silence.

"What?" came eventually.

"What...?" I took a deep breath. "What are you going to do...to me?"

"Nothing bad, I hope."

"You 'hope'?" But I didn't get an answer, and I was left alone in the dark.

* * *

Time ticks slowly when you're waiting for the unexpected to leap out at you from the darkness of a strangely quiet house. I held my breath until I thought I would burst.

And then something occurred to me.

I could escape now while they weren't with me. But how would I find the door…?

I heard a clatter.

I held my breath, my heart leaping frantically. Then, out of nowhere, someone grabbed my wrist and yanked me to my feet. They dragged me carelessly across the house.

A lamp came on. And revealed a scene I wish I could unsee.

Chapter 47

I shook in fright as I looked around the room.

"Are you watching, human?" Contrarietas asked. I couldn't answer. "What do you think of our little charade? Tell me. *I'd love to know,"* came her dark tone. But I had no words for the so perfectly-planned quiet deaths of everyone in the room. "If you were paying attention outside," she continued, "I came to their door and I asked them if they would let me in, for a ferocious animal was after me!" she expressed dramatically. "At that moment, Facetus was in fact the 'ferocious animal' after me, making a racket for evidence—and to distract the policemen, a win-win." She said it so casually, but so disturbing was the situation….

I slowly looked at Facetus. Even after all this time, I still couldn't believe he'd been a part of something like this. "And these stupid, unknowing humans had no clue!" How could she say that in such glee? "And now look what happened to them. Tsk, tsk, tsk," she said playfully.

Facetus didn't look at me once as I watched him stare at the floor. Hazley—at least, I *think* that little vampire was her—walked to him, stepping over poor souls as she went. He took notice of her, and they both looked in my direction. It was all very eerie; not just their stare, but *them* in general.

Sleek black creatures with nearly flat, yet convex, faces, and claws that looked nearly a foot long. I looked to my left and saw the same thing there, and jumped back in fright as shiny black eyes stared above a crooked grin of razor-sharp teeth.

I hit the ground and my neck bent backward with the impact, and I felt the piercing pain—worse than ever—in my head from where I'd hit it on the bathroom sink earlier. I groaned and tried to put myself upright.

I felt something brush my right arm.

I screamed as I looked up. "No no no no. Shh shh shh shh." I heard Facetus's voice, but I only saw a demonic animal. He extended one of his clawed hands—or was it a foot? He was on all fours now—toward my face. I repelled away. And so he moved it closer to me. I hated the suspension. Couldn't he just claw me and get it over with?

"She's not going to do it," I heard Contrarietas say, but I didn't take my eyes off his blades for fingers. And that's when I noticed they weren't as long as before. In fact, I could see the claws shrinking by the second. And soon they were smooth and flat. And then his fingers looked softer and lightened in color.

I slowly looked up. And I found Facetus. Bangs framing amber-colored eyes and everything. And now it wasn't knives meeting my skin, it was a person's hand offering help. But I couldn't take it. Not after what I'd seen. Didn't he know that? So I waited for him to be the one to break the silence.

"I won't hurt you," he murmured.

"You're wasting my time!" Contrarietas yanked me to my feet. She was still a vampire, and I was really wishing I'd taken Facetus's hand so that I could be with him right now instead of her.

I started hyperventilating, little squeaks of fear escaping me. "You're scaring her," Facetus said. He looked at Hazley, and she started turning human.

"Of course. That's what we're supposed to be doing," Contrarietas said bitterly. "It's great fun to watch a weak stupid human shake in fear, it's entertaining to hear them scream as they realize they're nothing compared to us," she laughed lightly.

The other vampires didn't say anything. Hazley was watching Facetus, and he was watching Contrarietas.

"Ugh. You're both so annoying." She threw me to the ground.

As I struggled to get back up from the startling fall, I heard a noise that was somewhere between a yowl and a growl. I paused and held my breath in fear.

Silence.

I stayed frozen for a minute before looking up. Facetus was looking at me. Contrarietas and Hazley were nowhere in sight. I looked back at Facetus. His eyes were closed. I carefully stood up. His eyes flew back open. He stared into me. He was human, but he was close enough that he could attack me on a dime. I shivered.

"Do you want to go to another room?" he asked me.

I looked around the room out of a horror film.

"You can't leave this house but you can go to another room," he said. I slowly turned back to him. I nodded slowly, dropping my eyelids. I didn't want to look at anything right now—particularly here.

And so, he led me away somewhere. And let me tell you, it is not pleasant to nearly trip over a dead body.

He led me up the stairs and eventually up a ladder.

"Nothing happened here," he said. I looked around the dusty attic illuminated by the moon.

I sat in an old chair and breathed the musty air. I examined the floorboards for a few moments, then I almost had to force myself out of curiosity to see what Facetus was doing. He looked bored as he stared at me and stared....

"Fa...," I began. His eyes opened a bit more. "Fa...Facetus...is something bad going to happen to me? Will I ever get to go home and see Marcie again, or will I be here forever—"

"I don't know," he simply said.

"Why do you do all of this?" I could feel the tears rolling down my face. "Why do you—to all these people and—how—how—I don't—" I had to stop.

I opened my eyes in surprise as I felt a hand brushing away my tears. Facetus had come over and was now sitting on the arm of the chair. "It's not that I want to," he said. "If I had the choice, I wouldn't. I only kill for food, but I can't."

I didn't understand—especially that last part. "Wha—"

"Will you stay here?" he asked, getting up. I nodded.

I wondered where he was going to go. *Probably to Contrarietas and Hazley,* I thought.

"Good," he said.

I waited for him to open the attic hatch, but he never did. Instead, not too far from the chair, he crouched down and curled up into a ball, his eyes closed. *Like an animal,* I thought. Well, that *was* what he was. An animal indeed. And to be honest, he often reminded me of a dog.

I watched his middle expand and collapse slowly until I thought I would fall asleep myself.

Chapter 48

I sat up with a start as a *thud* sounded. And not long after, it was followed by more.

The attic door swung open. Emerged a girl I'd never seen before. But I didn't have to wonder long about who she was.

"Get up, Facetus!" she growled as she kicked him in the stomach. He groaned and rolled over. "Come on, I haven't all night!"

Hazley's head poked up through the hatch. That's when I noticed she and Contrarietas looked very similar, except Contrarietas had darker hair while Hazley's was lighter like Facetus's. Maybe they don't have very many blueprints when it comes to looking like a human.

Contrarietas looked at me. "Get up, human!" she demanded.

I obeyed, springing to my feet. Almost too fast because I wobbled.

"Come." She jerked me down the attic steps. Facetus and Hazley followed. She dragged me through the house until we reached the back door. She paused, looking at me carefully. "Hmm…I don't think I should kill you yet," she said. "No, I'm not done playing with you yet." Her eyes blackened. I jolted away from her, but she had a hold on my wrist, so it was no use. Her eyes turned back to human blue and she laughed. "Oh, I love it when they do that!"

Facetus and Hazley said nothing as we passed through the trees—they barely made any noise at all. Contrarietas, on the other hand, was in great glee over my struggles in the extremely dark forest.

Eventually, Contrarietas stopped dragging me and sternly said, "Don't fall asleep this time." Then she finally let go of me.

"I won't," I heard Facetus's voice say. Then she and Hazley traveled deeper into the forest—or at least, by what I could hear. "I'm going...to take you," Facetus sighed.

"Take me where?" I asked.

"Come on." I felt his arm close around my waist, and soon I couldn't feel the ground under my feet anymore.

I guessed we were—well, *he* was—climbing because there many pauses and more jumps to follow. Eventually we stopped. Facetus was out of breath.

After a moment of panting, he led me somewhere

across the rock. "Here, climb this. It's not hard," he said.

I blindly pulled myself up a few feet of jagged rock sticking out of the mountain. When I reached the end, it was flat. I tried to stand up but hit my head on something, so I continued crawling until I was completely in the little nook. A bit of moonlight finally shone and I saw Facetus come up into the hole with me. We were both leaning against the smooth wall of rock when I—amazingly—broke the silence.

"Are you tired?" He had been very quiet and still. "Do you want to sleep? I'll wake you up when she comes back." I honestly felt a little bad for him.

"No, it's fine," he mumbled. "I'm sorry…you have to go through all this."

I didn't know how to answer that. After all, he was the one who'd brought me here in the first place!

"I can't let anything happen to Hazley," he said. "And if you had told the police, I—" He sighed.

"Why can't you let anything happen to her?" This conversation was going surprisingly well.

"Because she—" He sighed again. "I love her so much and she's my…." I didn't understand the end as his mumbling became incoherent. I guessed with fatigue.

"What? She's your what?" I was very curious.

He sighed and said nothing. "I'm supposed to say 'like,' aren't I?" he said after a moment.

"What?"

"Like. I'm supposed to say I like Hazley. Or is it 'love'? I don't know." Silence. "How are you?"

"I'm…not good," I said.

"How do you feel?"

"I-I'm afraid of what's going to happen, if I'm even going to live to tomorrow, your friends…you." I waited for him to get mad, but he stayed quiet. "I'm sad…that it's all come to this"—my voice broke—"and—and mostly that it's you. You of all people, and I—I feel lonely, scared, and—and hurt…." That didn't begin to express my feelings, but I didn't have any other words.

I heard sniffing right by my ear. I leaned away in surprise. I tried to see in the dark, but it was difficult. I raised my arm slowly and my hand hit Facetus in a second. I lowered my arm just as slowly. Seconds later, I heard sniffing again. I jolted back again. "Why are you smelling me?"

"You said you were hurt," he said. As if that made sense.

"Yeah…?"

"So, I'm…." I could actually feel his face on my arm this time.

I jumped back. "Stop it! It's weird!"

"I don't understand," he said.

"It's weird to smell someone!"

"But…I'm helping you."

"Helping me? You're smelling me!"

He was silent.

"And how are you helping me? No, you're doing the opposite of that! You're the reason I'm up here! You're the reason I'm going to die! You're the reason I'm hurting! You're the reason for—"

I heard a high-pitched whine. Must've been some animal in the trees or something.

"You're the reason for everything," I finished. "And I actually *liked* you—dare I say *love*—but now, after everything you've done…I don't think I've ever meant it more when I say: I hate you. I literally hate you. For who you are and everything you've done. I hate you."

I heard that whining sound again, only it wasn't distant this time; it sounded much closer. And it wasn't just one, it was prolonged. I wondered what it could be.

It sounded like it was just outside the cave—or whatever we were in. Or even, just inside. I couldn't tell. And then, just as instantly as it had started, it was gone.

Chapter 49

In the silence that followed, I questioned myself on whether I really hated him or was just mad. I mean, *hate* is such a strong word. But no matter how much I pondered it, I still had no sure answer. A voice startled me out of my thoughts.

"Come on, human!" Contrarietas yanked me out. I shrieked as she grabbed my injured arm. I gasped in pain as she finally let go. *"Well?"* she said as if she was expecting something.

"She's blind," I heard Facetus say.

"What?"

"She's blind in the dark," he said. "She can't see."

Contrarietas groaned. "You weak stupid humans, you're completely useless! Well, not always…." I could almost hear her evil smirk. "Hazley…."

"She's had enough!" Facetus said.

I heard a low growling. *"I say* when she's had enough!" Now there was a great deal of growling and even some snarling. I felt goosebumps as I listened.

The growling became louder and more aggressive. I heard a faint whining, but I couldn't tell where it was coming from. Then, out of nowhere, I heard a sharp hiss.

Then the rest of the night sounds were drowned out by snarling and hissing. I didn't know whether it would be safer to try to get away or to stay put in the loudest darkness I'd ever experienced.

That whining sound became louder, and I could've sworn it was right next to me. Then it stopped.

"No see?"

I recognized the voice as Hazley's. "I can't see." I don't know why I answered her. Maybe it was because I couldn't see her, and so to me she was just a beautiful, gentle tone.

"You can see?"

"No."

A moment later, I felt a hand on my—uninjured— arm, and somebody with the gentlest touch led me somewhere. We stopped. I waited. "Jump," Hazley said, letting go of me.

"Jump?" I didn't understand.

"Jump."

I wasn't entirely certain, but her calm tone and gentleness led me to belief and I did. And I fell.

And I screamed and screamed. Why had I listened to her? Then, just like before, someone caught me at the end of the fall. Only, it wasn't Facetus this time. It was someone much more fragile and littler.

Hazley dropped me to my feet. I had no words, breathless as I was. Then that whining started again.

"What is that?" I asked as I caught my breath.

"What?" Hazley breathed. The noise had stopped just as she'd answered.

"That high-pitched sound." I mimicked it. "What is it?"

"I'm scared," she answered. It's amazing to think those horrific creatures were capable of fear; although when it comes to Hazley, it would be odd to think of her as *not* afraid. She always seemed so timid, and I always wondered why.

Then that noise started again.

"Really, what is that?" I asked again.

She didn't answer, and I felt a chill as I listened. It wasn't the wind; I had no idea what was making that sound—or if it was dangerous or not.

"Hazley?" I asked fearfully. "What is that? Are we in danger? Do we need to get out of here?" All the words were coming out fast and jumbled. "Hazley?"

"What?" she squeaked.

"Are we in danger? Are we—" I noticed the sound

had stopped again.

"What?" she asked.

"It stopped," I said, listening carefully.

"What? Stop what?"

"The noise. It stopped." I strained my ears but all I could hear were crickets.

"No noise," she said after a pause.

"Yeah, not anymore," I said, but I still wasn't entirely satisfied. "What do you think it was?"

"What?"

"The noise. What do you think it was?"

"I no like noise," she said.

"I know, but"—actually, I didn't know, but I was getting frustrated and anxious—"what do you think that noise was? What kind of animal made that? Are we in danger?"

It took her a moment to answer. "Humans," she said.

"No, I mean—" I sighed.

A shriek echoed through the night. It didn't sound human; it sounded very animal like.

I heard a whimper followed by whining. "Hazley?" I said frantically.

"What?" Her words were smothered in squeak.

"It's you!" I exclaimed. "It's you who's making the noise, isn't it?"

But we were interrupted by more screaming. And then Hazley—I think—started screaming. And I freaked out. If she was screaming, it must be bad. I looked around, hoping to catch sight of whatever beast was coming, but try as I might, it was simply just too dark.

Chapter 50

The screaming stopped, and Hazley did too. I cautiously listened for any sign of immediate danger. But other than the crickets, all was silent, and the wind was still. It was so quiet, in fact, that I wasn't sure if Hazley was still here with me or not. "H-Hazley?" I asked quietly. Just in case there was a creature in the darkness, I didn't want it to hear us. "Hazley?" I asked frantically when she didn't answer.

"What?" she whimpered.

"What's wrong?" She sounded so upset I actually felt worried for her. "What? What is it?"

"I'm scared," she replied.

"Why? Why are you scared?" I struggled to not flip out too much and to calmly and slowly ask her, but I managed.

She didn't answer.

"Hazley, what is it? Why are you scared?" I thought of something. "Were you scared earlier? I could hear whimpering when I was with Facetus." Silence. "Were you scared when I was with Facetus?"

"No...," she said. "I scared fight."

"You're scared of a fight? But...." Well, if that wasn't

Hazley earlier, then what was it?

"Come on, Hazley! Why'd you bring the human down here?" I hadn't known Contrarietas had come down. She scoffed. "Why am I even adjusting to *your* needs?" Then she stopped talking and started making animal noises instead.

I had no clue what was going on. I heard Hazley whimper again. Then I heard a thud and a grunt over my shoulder. I veered around quickly, scared stiff. I then heard deep breathing not far from where I stood. I myself couldn't find my own breath in fear.

I heard the breathing come closer then move past me. Hazley whined softly. I wondered fearfully what it was.

More animal noises sounded, Hazley continued to whine, and I was utterly clueless as to what was going on. I felt like crying again from fear.

Hazley's whining ceased as the animal noises stopped, and I heard the quiet steps of someone walking away. Then all was silent and still. I heard a sigh. My senses perked up as I listened for more. I shivered, scared and anxious. After a moment or two, I heard a soft squeak. I bet it was Hazley. I mean, who else would it be?

In the dim moonlight, I thought I could see something. *I wonder what it coul—oh god, it just moved! Oh, it just—Oh...!*

My breathing accelerated and my pulse quickened. *What was it? Was it Contrarietas? Facetus? Hazl—*

I heard another sigh, and if I'm not mistaken, it came from whoever—or *what*ever—that creature was. It—I think—grunted. "I'm sorry, Maybeline, O.K.?" It was Facetus. And he sounded mad. "But I don't care about you anymore, so...."

I waited for him to finish, but he didn't. Instead, he whined softly. His whine sounded different than Hazley's....

"It was you!" I exclaimed with realization. "It was *you* who wa—"

I stopped quickly in thought and jumped as I heard a loud bark behind me. This was followed by more growls and grunts—that I guessed to be Contrarietas's. When she—I think—stopped, I was startled by something that touched my back. It had a different feel as it nudged me forward; rougher than Facetus but gentler than Contrarietas. I wondered who it was.

The hand in the dark didn't lead me far. When we

stopped, it simply just dropped and left me alone, no instructions or anything.

Just seconds later, I heard some strange noises. I also heard an occasional growl. It took me some minutes, but I'd finally deducted that they were either making weird noises to attract prey, or they had already caught their prey and were eating it. Such a shame they didn't eat the humans—I mean, I'd rather they not, but they're such wasteful creatures that way.

I wondered why they kept growling. Maybe my theories were wrong because that detail didn't seem to fit with either of them.

Then I heard some scraping sounds and what sounded like the snapping of plastic…or something like that. The scraping soon stopped, but the snapping and cracking continued. I wondered what they were doing.

The cracking stopped. But all wasn't silent for even a moment. One of the vampires started growling, then another joined in—kind of like what it had sounded like on the cliff top. I wonder, do they fight a lot? Hazley must have a hard time then. No wonder she never looks happy.

Only, instead of them breaking into a vicious—or at

least, what it *sounded* like—match, it ceased. So much time had passed that I'd actually gotten it in my head that there was a possibility they'd forgotten about me. No such luck.

I heard the creature moving toward me before it reached me. I knew I stood no chance, but I quickly turned on my heel anyway.

Dawn.

Chapter 51

There was just enough light creeping over the horizon that I could see just the right distance ahead of me to avoid running into and tripping over stuff.

I knew they would catch me in the end, but something inside me told me to keep going at all costs. I didn't want to stop running—I *couldn't* stop running—but I knew I'd be much faster without my shoes. So, stumbling through a bit of a gallop as I groped at the straps of my heels, I managed to kick them off and take off at full speed.

And...*ow,* that hurt a lot! No time to complain now; *run, Chevy, run!*

I can't believe it! I'm actually going to make—
Well, I almost did.

I screamed and kicked as I struggled against... whoever it was who had a firm grasp on me. It wasn't long before the lock on me collapsed. It was surprising, but I didn't waste time thinking about it. Instead, I ran out of the trees and into the sunlight.

I quickly glanced around, taking in my surroundings. An old pickup in a field caught my eye. As a kid, I liked to joke that I owned a truck company because of my last name, but now was no joking matter. I bolted for it. But someone beat me to it.

I tried to quickly stop and change course, but he was faster. He leaped toward me and knocked me to the ground. I tried my best, but he had me pinned in such a way that I couldn't escape. Not even a little. I even found it a little hard to breathe as he was sitting on my stomach, staring down at me. I couldn't move my legs, and he was holding on to both of my wrists with one hand, so I couldn't do anything with those either. His other hand was the only part of him that wasn't human, poised with its razor-sharp claws extended, ready to hit me—and probably kill me too.

"No! No, Facetus, listen," I said anxiously. "Listen, I-I have something to tell you…before you kill me." I was talking as fast as I could in that moment of limited breath, and my mind was racing faster than ever. He paused. Good. Keep stalling. "I-I was lying earlier when I said"—I gasped as his grip on my wrists tightened—"when I said that…. I didn't mean it when I said…I hated you. I was just mad. I still love you and I always will." And as I said it, I realized it was true. "I love you, Facetus."

He cocked his head to the side, trying to decide

whether or not to believe me.

"Please. Please, Facetus, please. I love you, I do…." I had no idea what I was saying now; I was just babbling. "Please…." I'd better figure out what I was saying please to because I was running out of breath.

"Please…," I barely made out. His grip on my wrists slowly loosened until he'd let go completely and he lowered his clawed hand, looking at me all the while. I couldn't say any more to him; I was out of breath.

I couldn't tell him to get off me and I couldn't push him off either. I barely even felt the strength to move at all. I slowly closed my eyes because at this point it was so tiring to keep them open.

A second went by, and I felt something on my face.

I barely managed to force my eyes open. It was Facetus. He rubbed his nose against mine. I looked at him, gasped, and started coughing. How amazing that rush of fresh air felt, I can't describe. He hovered above me, staring right back.

Still panting, I slid my elbows under me. He pulled me up to my feet. I stared at him in gratitude. But that moment didn't last long.

Some force yanked me away from Facetus, and I was suddenly facing Contrarietas. Odd, she was human....

"Thought you would get away, huh?" she said to me. "Think again." She bared her sharp teeth. I whimpered and shook with fear. But just before she sank them into me or whatever she planning to do, something pulled me back from her and held me tightly.

"No, don't kill her," I heard Facetus's voice say by my ear. "Please, Contrarietas."

She snarled, but he didn't let go of me. She started growling and then ran toward us in fury. Facetus shoved me away from him, and I didn't look back to see what happened next. Instead, I got to my feet and glanced around quickly. I could still go to that truck. I could lock the doors so they can't get in! I ran up the hill to it.

I swung open the passenger door, which was closer, and jumped in. I closed the door and locked it, then climbed to the driver side. I locked that door as well.

Miraculously, I happened to look down and see the key lying in the console. I quickly grabbed it and put it in the ignition. There are so few people out here, the farmer who owns this must not be afraid of someone stealing it.

I started it up and drove to what I hoped would be freedom.

Chapter 52

I had no idea what the speed limit was, but I just kept pumping the gas, trying to go as fast as I could. The sooner I got out, the better.

Just as I had left the farmhouses behind, a raccoon ran out into the road. I quickly slammed on the brakes. The truck jolted to a stop. I looked around. It wasn't anywhere in sight and I hadn't felt the truck hit anything.

Confused, I slowly backed up. Had it all been in my imagination? There was nothing on the road in front of me. *Odd,* I thought.

I heard a slight tap. Must have been the wind or something hitting the metal of the truck. I put it in drive and started on my mission again.

It wasn't long before I was scared out of my wits.

I heard that tapping sound again. It sounded like it was coming from the roof. I barely had any time to wonder though, because suddenly, it jumped down on the windshield.

I shrieked in both surprise and fear and hit the gas pedal to go faster. It still did not move though, pressing itself against the windshield and staring at me with its glossy black eyes.

Then, I did something I'd never done before. Still trying to get the truck to exceed its limit, I stomped on the brake with my other foot. The truck locked up, and the thing flew off the windshield and landed on the road in front of me.

I had to quickly make a decision. Either way I went would lead me to danger; the vampire in front of me, or the other vampires on the stretch of road behind.

I could tell this vampire was male—he was built like Facetus, not petite like Hazley or Contrarietas—but he was not Facetus. I don't know how I could tell; I just knew.

Either way I went, I needed to drive. I tried moving the truck, but it wouldn't budge. I messed with the key, but still, it kept stalling.

Oh no no no no no no no no. No, it had to go! It needed to go! *I* needed to go!

The vampire had gotten back up and was making its way toward me.

I had no choice.

I jumped out and ran—maybe two steps. It grabbed me and threw me back toward the truck. "Well, well, well. Where do you think you're going?" it asked as it held me against the side of the vehicle.

A girl dropped out of the sky and said, "Well, Tribulatio, what do we have here?"

"We got a little runner," he said.

"You should probably turn human," she said. "I hear the police have been out here, and we wouldn't want trouble, would we?"

"Trouble's my middle name," he said as he changed. They said everything with a hint of amusement, like it was some kind of joke.

They both had the whitest skin I'd even seen. He had darker than dark black hair, while hers was a flaming red. Both colors accented their paleness.

"What are we going to do with her?" she asked.

"Whatever we want," he replied. They both grinned wickedly at me.

"No! Please, let me go!" I said frantically. "Please!" I started crying.

"Oh, is the wittle girl scared?" he asked tauntingly.

"Don't worry. We'll take good care of you," she said.

"No! Let me go! Let me—" I struggled against him. "Facetus!" I screamed.

"What did you say?" He stopped fighting me. It was no longer a joke; they were both staring at me.

"Let me go," I said, hoping the impossible would happen.

"No no no. After that."

"After?" I thought. "I yelled for…my friend."

"Who's your friend?" she asked me.

"Fa…Facetus," I said. "That's his name."

They both looked at each other, then he let me go.

Chapter 53

I stared incredulously at them. I began edging away.

"How do you know him?" she asked.

"I-I met him…," I said shakily, still backing away, "at work…."

"Facetus has a job?" he asked.

"N-no, I don't think so," I said. "It was at my work."

"Is that so?"

I nodded. But when I looked back, they were gone.

I quickly looked around, trying to figure out where they'd gone.

"Oh, are you lost? Let me find you."

I turned to see Contrarietas behind me. I barely had time to say or do anything before she pounced on me.

I screamed, "Facetus!"

"Oh, you think he's going to help you now? You probably wouldn't even recognize him with his entrails hanging out." She grinned evilly, flashing her shiny teeth. I gasped in sorrow. She laughed. "He should've known better than to fight me. He knows very well how much stronger I am. He must have really cared about you," she said with fake sympathy. "Too bad his effort had no use." She smiled and ejected her claws.

I closed my eyes, waiting for the impact. Instead, I felt the weight get lifted off me. I opened my eyes and sat up.

"You always were bad at lying." Facetus was alive! "I liked that about you."

The two broke into combat, clawing at each other and snarling viciously. I couldn't watch. I squeezed my eyes shut, praying that it would end soon.

I could hear the fight getting more intense, their snarls getting louder and even a scream here and there.

Suddenly, the snarls died out as a loud *snap* sounded in the air.

I slowly opened my eyes.

I saw what I thought was Contrarietas lying limp on the ground. I looked up and saw Hazley and the two vampires I'd met minutes ago. There was not a bit of fear on their faces as they looked at Facetus with surprise as he stared in shock at what he'd done.

I rose to my feet. All their heads instantly went my direction. Was I really that loud? Maybe to them.

Facetus looked back to Contrarietas and they all

looked back at him. All was silent. He looked awful. His face was covered with scratches along with the rest of his body. His expression was…sad? Regretful? I couldn't tell.

Like he could hear my thoughts, he looked at me and told me with his eyes he was hurt. I wasn't sure why though. I tried to transit "Why?" back, but I didn't get a solid reply.

His eyes dropped to Contrarietas for a split second before looking out into the distance. Then, he raced away somewhere into the thicket.

The two other vampires looked at Hazley. She stared back at them. The boy walked up to her. He rubbed noses with her before kissing her. The red-haired girl then did the nose-rub, but she didn't kiss her. I knew kissing was what you did with friends, but what did the nose-rub mean?

After some time, the vampires spoke to me, asking my name and how I'd befriended Facetus. They told me their names were Tribulatio and Tenebris. It turned out Contrarietas had thought they were dead along with the rest of the vampire population. Facetus had protected them, making sure she didn't find out. He had done a lot for them actually, along with many others before. He'd always fought with Contrarietas, but they never actually thought he'd kill her one day. Tenebris even said she had never known anyone to kill their own mate. Shocked, I was about to ask her what she meant, but then Facetus came back.

I'd never seen him like this before. I wondered, had he been crying? The look in his eyes was so distant.

Hazley rushed to his side and snuggled up against him. He looked at her and they rubbed heads. It bothered me I didn't know what they were saying.

Tenebris ran up and kissed him, then she rubbed noses. Facetus and Tribulatio simply looked at each other for a second without a word or primitive touch. Facetus looked at Contrarietas.

"I'll do it," Tribulatio said. Facetus looked back at him. "I will."

They turned around. I looked to see what they saw. A police car was in the distance, traveling in our direction. It didn't have its lights flashing or sirens going; I recognized it by its colors.

Tenebris and Tribulatio quickly took Contrarietas away somewhere. Facetus approached Hazley, placing his hands on her shoulders. He kissed her, then looked in her eyes. "You go have fun. But be a good girl, O.K.?"

She nodded. "I love you, Facetus," she said.

"I love you too, my beautiful daughter," he answered, smiling.

What?

She smiled and ran off.

Chapter 54

When the police car approached us, the officer stopped and got out. He began to question us on what was going on, why was Facetus covered head to toe in claw marks?

We told him a partially true story. We were out and about when we were attacked by this wild animal—we didn't recognize what it was. We saw this pickup and saw it as our only chance of escape. The creature got ahead of us and we accidentally hit it. Then it limped off into the forest—Oops, we don't remember which way it went!

The policeman gave us a ride back to the city. I decided I would just go get my car later.

Facetus and I got out of the back seat and walked up to the apartment building.

"You know…." I paused. Facetus looked at me. "I—I actually meant it when, uh, when I said I…when I said I loved you."

"I know," he said. He paused. "Don't you mean 'like'?"

"No," I said. "I love you. You're a wonderful friend…." *Most of the time,* I guiltily thought.

"I thought you say 'like' to friends."

"You do. It depends on the friendship."

"So, you say 'love' to…mates and *some* friends?"

"Special friends," I said. "As in, the ones you can't live without."

He just smiled. He looked down. "What happened to your arm? Did Cont—" He broke off.

"No," I simply said.

He looked back up. "Did I…?"

I avoided eye contact and slowly nodded.

"Oh, I'm sorry, baby," he said.

I looked at him. He really *was* sorry. I could see it on his face.

He touched my arm gently, looking at me. "I won't hurt you," he said as he raised my arm. I have to admit it made me nervous to have him messing with my injured arm, but I stayed quiet.

He bent his head down and started licking my cuts. "The neighbors might see!" I said with a bit of a laugh in my voice. His tongue tickled a little.

He dropped my arm, satisfied, and we went inside.

"There she is! Well, it's about time!" Mr. Rockwell said.

"What are you yelling about now!" Ms. Fellers

bellowed in response.

"This *girl* went out last night and she never came back. Now here she is with her boyfriend, wearing the same clothes as she was yesterday when she left! I tell you, it's suspicious! Young people are doing it too early nowadays!"

"Mr. Rockwell…!" I'd never been more embarrassed by the elderly.

"Why are you talking to those carpets?" Ms. Fellers screeched.

"They're not carpets, they're—"

While the two of them bickered, Facetus and I made our way to the stairs. He barely made it to the top. I hadn't realized how injured he was. I helped him up them, which wasn't an easy task, but not all things should be easy when you really care about someone, right? I really wanted to ask him about Hazley and Contrarietas, but I guessed the topic might be a little sensitive, so I didn't. When we reached my floor, I also noticed he had a slight limp in his walk.

When we reached my door, he surprised me.

He stared at me for a moment, then slowly leaned over to kiss me, and then pulled me in a hug—like, a *real* hug. Not a you're-hugging-me-so-I-have-to-hug-you hug, but an actual hug.

After a few minutes, he released me and the hug ended. I smiled at him. He smiled back. I jumped up to hug him again.

"O.K....," he said, pulling away.

"Why don't you like hugs?" I asked.

"It means something different to us than it does to you," he said slowly. "But I figure, the amount you let me kiss you, you deserve a hug."

"Oh," I said. "What does a hug mean to you?"

"It means...." His face twisted in disgust. Either that, or dread. "It means...you want to...*mate*...with someone."

"Oh." I smiled awkwardly. He smiled back.

I had the feeling this was the start of a truly beautiful friendship.

Keep reading for a sneak peek of the next book in the series, **One Strange Christmas.**

Chapter 1

"Hey!"

"Hey!" I answered.

"What's going on?" Marcie asked me as she shut the door behind her.

"So...I may or may not have forgotten about my grandma's birthday and now I have to make dozens of cupcakes, but it'll be fine. It'll be fine," I laughed, trying to sound breezy, but I certainly didn't feel that way.

"When were you supposed to make them?"

"Like, I don't know, *ages ago!*" I probably should have made them last weekend.

"So...Mr. Saperstien was O.K. with you missing work?"

Mr. Saperstien.

"Oh my god, I forgot!" I said, reaching for my phone. I got a bunch of flour on it, but that doesn't matter, right? No? Yes. Now none of the buttons work.

"Well, I'd help you, but I've got an exam coming up, so I need to study for that." She headed off down the hall.

Of course. I mean, it's great Marcie's a dedicated student and all, but sometimes it can be annoying—

like when I need help, for instance!

I added the final ingredient—blueberries—and turned the electric mixer on one last time. Marcie had received it as a graduation gift, but this was its first time ever being used.

After I turned the mixer off, I found that I couldn't get the bowl out. Oh no! I looked at the clock. I didn't have much time left. I started shaking it in panic, and surprisingly, it worked.

All right, now I have to lift the bowl and pour the mixture into the cupcake tins. My arms were wobbling. Either I was going to end up dropping this or making a mess or both.

"Facetus!" I called. No answer. "Ugh," I said in frustration. "Facetus, come here! I need help." No answer.

Annoyed, I slammed the bowl down on the counter and marched into the living room.

Facetus, my best friend next to Marcie, was curled up in a blanket on the couch.

"Facetus." I'd barely touched him when he suddenly hissed and tackled me. "I need help in the kitchen," I said, like it's normal for him to throw me to the floor. Because it was. He does it every time I wake him up. He can't help it; it's in his instincts.

He got off me and trudged into the kitchen.

"Can you pick up this bowl and pour the batter into the cups?" I asked. "But don't get any on the pan."

"What cups?" he asked, looking around.

"These." I pointed to the cupcake wrappers cushioned in the pans. "A different kind of cup," I explained.

"In the paper things?" he asked, picking the bowl up.

"Yes," I answered.

I was impressed. He didn't get any batter anywhere else but in the cupcake holders. "Thanks," I said, picking one of the trays up. I wondered if I could fit them all in the oven.

I was sliding the last one in, trying to lean to fit it in just right, when I lost my balance.

I was about to go face first into the oven door, but Facetus caught me. He pulled me back from the oven and didn't let go of me until I'd planted both feet firmly on the ground.

My heart was still racing. "Thanks," I said.

"You're welcome," he said, putting his head on my shoulder. No, he's not my boyfriend. His entire family is that way. They like touching you to express themselves.

He paused and turned to me. "I don't think I've ever really seen you bake before."

"Yeah, well, today's my grandma's birthday so I have to make a bunch of cupcakes for her"—I looked at the clock—"that need to be ready *now,*" I whined.

"Why? Is she coming here?"

"No, but she lives so far away. Like, *two-hour* drive!"

"When do you have to be there?"

"By noon," I answered. "My mom's picking me up."

"Why didn't you make them earlier?"

"I forgot!" His questions were getting annoying.

Chapter 2

"You know, birthdays sound fun," Facetus said, crossing his arms and leaning back against the counter.

"Do you have one?" I blinked. "When is it?"

"I don't know," he shrugged. "I've never celebrated it."

"Well, we should celebrate yours sometime!" I said. "We'll make up a day, just for you!"

He nodded slowly. "But, don't you have to know how old I am?"

I shrugged. "We can still celebrate." Curiosity struck me. "How old are you, anyway?"

"Maybes, you know I don't know that," he said. "I don't think I even *want* to know that."

"Well, we'll just have your first birthday, then your second, and your third, and blah blah blah."

He pondered this. "My first birthday. I like the idea of being one."

"Are you full grown when you're one?" I asked. "Like dogs?"

He shrugged. "I don't know."

"Well, what about Hazley? How old was she when

she grew up?" Hazley is Facetus's daughter.

"I don't know!" He was getting annoyed, I could tell. But saved by the bell, the oven beeped. He kept talking though. "Besides, I was only there for half her childhood." I turned to him in surprise. "And it's not like I can ask…Contrarietas." Contrarietas was Hazley's mother. I only knew her briefly—she died this summer—but I can tell you that the woman was crazy. In fact, she tried to kill me. "Well, are you going to get the…the…!"

"Cupcakes?" I offered brightly, trying to soften the mood as I put on mitts.

"Whatever," he said.

"Would you mind helping me?" I asked sheepishly. "Again?"

He grumbled something unintelligible.

"Set this on the counter." I held out a tray behind me as I reached for more. An assembly line would be quicker; the cupcakes less likely to burn.

I heard him yelp behind me. "You're supposed to put mitts on," I told him. I set the tray on the counter myself and pointed to an extra pair of mitts.

"Here," I said as I tried to hand him the next pan. Never mind, assembly-line method is taking longer.

He had his mitts on, but he shook his head.

"Come on, Facetus, they're going to burn!" He still shook his head. "Look! I'm fine! The mitts protect your hands!" I was getting anxious. He shook his head again. I thrust the tray into his hand. He jumped back in fear, but soon realized that he was fine.

"There!" I said as I finally got the last tray out and closed the oven door.

"What's that?"

I turned and saw Facetus messing with some rectangle. He's so adorable, his face lit up like a little kid's as he fiddled with the device. The device that was my phone covered in flour.

Oh no.

"I forgot to call Mr. Saperstien!" I exclaimed. "Oh no oh no oh no!" I snatched my phone from his fingers. I brushed the flour off and dialed.

As I was waiting for him to pick up, I noticed Facetus had on a pouting face. "I have to call Mr. Saperstien," I whispered. "You can play with it later."

"Hi, Mr. Saperstien," I said when he picked up. "So...."

"Chevy! Where are you?"

"I know I know I know," I said. "Look, something

unexpected came up…."

"What?"

"My grandma's birthday."

"Uh huh."

"No, really, it's today!"

"And you call this 'unexpected'?"

"Please, Mr. Saperstien! Please please please!" I begged.

He sighed. "I worry about you, Chevy."

"Please!"

"You better be in tomorrow." He hung up.

I sighed in relief. But then I saw the clock. I screamed.

"What? What? Is someone bleeding?" Marcie rushed into the kitchen, first aid kit in hand.

"No, I just need to leave soon and—*oh no!*"

"What?" she and Facetus both said.

"Frosting! I forgot the frosting!" I threw open all the cupboards and the refrigerator. Finally I found a jar of plain cake frosting. "Yes!" I said. "Oh no!" Grandma is picky. She's not going to like store-bought. What to do? What to do?

I rummaged around again. I've got to add something so it doesn't taste store bought. Sugar!

Would more sugar work? Maybe, but Grandma might think it's too sweet. I've got to find something else! Why isn't anyone helping me! I turned around.

Facetus and Marcie were both giving me the same expression—an expression that told me they didn't understand what I was doing or why I was doing it.

"Hello!" I gestured to the cupboards.

They looked at each other, then back at me, still confused.

"Grandma doesn't like store-bought stuff!" I practically screamed.

They both came over to help me, but then Marcie remembered something. "I need to study!" she said, and rushed back down the hall.

Jewell Anne Sandy has spent her life reading all sorts of books and has been writing her own stories for as long as she can remember. Though she likes to be practical, she does very much enjoy imagining a world full of magic and mystical beings. Besides coming up with new plots and characters, she enjoys spending her time singing and dancing, along with enjoying the Midwestern weather of the United States.

Made in the USA
Columbia, SC
18 April 2021